SLAY ME

A DRAGONS LOVE CURVES NOVEL

AIDY AWARD

For my Dad who always, always supports me and tells me never to give up, even though I won't let him read the books.

Love bears all things, believes all things, hopes all things, endures all things. Love never fails…

~ Paul

DEAR FALLYN

*M*y fires,

From the first moment I saw you - when we were so young and naive - I knew you were mine. I knew I wanted nothing more than to belong to you.

Together we would change the world.

The world changed. But it wasn't because of our love.

Now, in these dark and dangerous times, you have nothing but hatred and fear in the depths of your soul for me.

My heart is broken. Broken for you, and all that you have suffered. Broken for me and everything we have lost, everything we have never had together.

I never wept. I never moaned for you in the night. Never once did I let the loss of you and the beauty our love could have been make me weak. I could never show my grief, my heartache.

Instead I built armor around my heart so no one would know, no one could see how losing you broke me. I have made a life without you. I am the alpha of alphas, the strongest of all Wyverns since the first sons. I am the Dragon Warrior all others fear. I do all of this your name.

A name I never thought I would say again. A name etched on my heart by the most painful time, a name I barely dared to think.

Until I saw you again for the first time in hundreds of years. Your name burned on my lips, the memories of you scorching my soul. A fire I thought long since dead, buried deep, sparked and ignited inside of me once again. Only when I called your name in the depths of Hell were you real to me.

Fallyn.

My Fallyn.

Damn you, Fallyn.

Why must you have such a stranglehold on my soul? Why do I need you so much it hurts? Why have you not been mine for all these dark years?

I will burn down the world to find you. Even if you and I are the only thing in existence not turned to ash, I would do it. To find you. To hold you. To show you my shattered wounded heart is yours and yours alone.

You may reject my offerings. You can slice my heart, my body, my soul with your blades, and still I will want and need only you. I have still never shed a tear, and my cold heart may never let me. But I have called out your name. When the night is the darkest and I wake having dreamt you were in my arms, your name slips from my mouth reaching no one's ears but my own with its mournful plea.

I am weak, nothing without you.

I cannot beg you to come to me, because you do not hear. I fear the only way we can be together is in Hell.

The final battle is coming. Good and evil will clash, and I

know you will be there. If it is the only time I have with you on this earth, I will take it. No other Dragon Warrior will battle more fiercely than I in hopes that by giving my all to defeat the forces of Hell, I can save you.

Even if you don't want to be saved.

That is my mission, my duty, my honor.

Then maybe you will be mine once again.

Until then.

Wieczni wierni,

--M

BE sure to read Match's book - the grand finale of the Dragons Love Curves series to find out what happens between Match and Fallyn.

DRAGON IN SHINING ARMOR

A hundred deaths would not appease the anger in Match's heart. He wore that anger like armor and used it to fuel his battle lust. He could kill a thousand more demon wyrms and just be getting warmed up. The darkness in his own soul, the taint every Red Dragon possessed, was just enough to keep him from any remorse over the death these pawns of the Black Dragon and the Queen of Hell suffered.

Tonight he was on the hunt, not because eviscerating the enemy would get him any closer to his goal, but because he needed to do something, anything besides sit on his ass in his lair. He'd had enough of healing. If one more of Zeleny's Green Dragons tried to play nursemaid to him, he was going to burn them to ashes instead of simply biting off their heads as he had been doing for the last month.

Which was exactly why he'd snuck out of his own home in the dead of night to slash his way through any demon wyrms he could find in the shadows. He was the alpha of alphas for dragonsake. This was the time for action, not strategy and planning. Not that his actions had gotten him anywhere except stabbed in the heart, taken on a wild goose chase, and poisoned.

Match beat his wings hard and soaring through the night sky, searched the land with the enhanced vision of his dragon. The little bastards knew better than to come too close the Red Dragon stronghold, but they were definitely nearby. How they'd gotten here, he didn't know, unless his subterranean tunnels had been discovered. There wasn't exactly a whole lot of volcanic activity in southern Poland. No volcanoes, no access to Hell. No Hell, no demons. Just the way he usually liked it.

Any normal Red Dragon would hate the cold snowy winters and the cool summer nights. Match was fond of the country his father had moved them to as a small boy. He had beautiful memories of his parents when he'd been very young taking him apple picking. Then the attack had happened, and he'd wanted nothing more than to leave Poland forever.

Somehow, he never could. His final memories of her were here.

Aha. The scent of acrid smoke wafted through the air. His prey were finally showing themselves. He swooped down toward the quiet town of Zywiec and spotted the little fuckers sneaking around the shadows of the local brewery. A little too close to home. Poisoning the beer would be the perfect way to spread their hateful plagues.

Not on his watch.

He used the wind to glide down silently and took out two demon wyrms from the back of the pack with his talons. The rest of them hadn't even noticed their brethren's deaths.

Dumb shits. They'd be easy to defeat if there weren't always so damn many of them. Fine. He was up for a bit of a challenge. He had a lot of pent up energy to burn off.

Of their faces.

Yes, melting the flesh from their sorry bones sounded quite fun. Perfect in fact for his first night out. Anger and boredom made great weapons.

Match roared just to give the enemy a scare and then swathed them in a long hot burst of fire. Half their numbers melted into puddles of black oily goo on the cobblestones of the courtyard. Ah, yes. That did feel good. He should have done this weeks ago.

There was nothing better for a broken heart than a good old-fashioned killing spree. Wait, not a broken heart. Bah. That was for whiner baby dragons not yet in their Prime. Match's heart was a cold dead thing, not a fragile fucking flower to be ripped apart and shredded by--

A pack of demon wyrms jumped away from a fireball aimed at their midst. Where the hell had that come from? Not him. Not one of these dumbasses. Another Red Dragon Warrior.

Fuck.

Busted.

Had to be either a babysitter or a young Warrior out to prove themselves. Just what he needed. He did not relish being scolded for not recovering at home in his bed or teaching the secrets of the Red Wyr to the younger up and coming Warriors. His job was to show the rest of his Wyr how to be the best among Dragons. That was something he'd been good at until recently.

Now was not the time to show weakness. He was the most

powerful alpha since the first sons of the First Dragon. Match roared again and sent out a mental call to his fellow shifter using his alpha voice, the one that could not be ignored.

Show yourself, brother. Come fight the demon horde head on with me.

More firebombs flew through the sky and into a demon wyrm who'd broken off from the others and was headed straight for Match, unnoticed. It exploded into chunky bits and one blackened piece plopped right onto his snout.

Sorry, boss. That was a good shot though, right? Dax Cervony swooped down off the roof of the brewery and sent a dozen more fireballs into the horde's center. As if he were a fucking red-breasted robin and not a dragon, he landed as light as a feather on the destroyed stones and shifted into his human form.

Any other Dragon Warrior and Match would send him packing. But Dax was the newly appointed second in command of the Red Wyr. Match had promoted the young Warrior to the position himself when he'd proven himself a talented and strong leader at Hell's attempt to steal the wolf and dragon babies.

The battle where she'd saved his life, touched his face, and told him he once again had to wait to find her.

Not yet.

Dammit, he didn't need her soft voice in his mind distracting him. That's how Dragons lost their heads. Literally.

Match looked around, didn't see any more wyrms he could destroy and shifted too. "Yes, it was a good shot. I like the fire-ball method you're using to target individuals. That could come in handy. Be sure to schedule time to teach that to our Warriors."

Dax called the fire element up from the smoldering flames of the dead and used it to shoot off another volley into the shadows where a new horde was forming. Damn. The wyrms might be stupid as shit, but they weren't dumb enough to keep coming when they couldn't even get out of hell in the first place. There went Match's night of fun and games. "What are you doing here, Second?"

"Trying to let you have some fun. But I'm pretty sure it's in my job description to keep your ass alive, so I intervened a little." He shrugged and folded his arms like he didn't have a care in the world. Except he didn't take his eyes off Match for a minute.

First Dragon above save him from well-meaning Warriors. Match kept his sigh and eyeroll to himself. "You aren't going to tell me I shouldn't be out here without my nanny and a pack of guards to protect me from everyone's favorite assassin?"

Dax yawned. "Nope."

"Why not?" Not that Match was sorry, but while he trusted Dax with his life, they hadn't worked side by side like he had with his last Second and didn't know every thought and move of this younger Warrior. So far, he liked Dax's leadership style and the way he left well-enough alone. This could be just the break he needed. After tonight, Match would leave the Wyr in Dax's hands and head out to search for his mate once again. After one last test. "What happened to keeping my ass alive?"

Dax didn't cower, he didn't even stand up straighter under Match's glare. He threw another fireball that loopty-looped in

the air over their heads and took out an escapee wyrm from
hell. "I figure you're the Wyvern and you've been alive a
crapton of a lot longer than me, not that I'm calling you old or
anything. And also, because you're safe from everyone's
favorite assassin, as you call her, for the moment."

Confident little jerk, wasn't he? He'd do just fine in
command of the Red Dragon Warriors. "Don't be getting
cocky. If she wants to slice me open some more, she will."

"Oh, I don't doubt that one bit. She's the sneakiest sneak
that ever sneaked." Dax looked a little too impressed by that.
"It's just that she isn't after you right this second."

"How do you know that?" Match's heart sped up, antici-
pating her attack. It would be just like her to make them feel
safe and then slip a dagger to the base of his throat.

He shrugged, very nonchalantly, and tipped his head in the
direction of the Red Dragon stronghold. "Because she's back
at the house waiting for you in your office."

What

The

Actual

Fuck?

Match shifted back to dragon form in a flash and flew
hard to get to the Red Dragon stronghold as fast as his wings
could carry him. He cursed Cage, all Gold Dragons, and the
wind for not helping him fly faster.

The estate came into view and the sky around him glowed
a deep crimson red. She was here, in his home. Waiting
for him.

There must be some mistake. He was supposed to go out
and find her. He was supposed to protect her. He wasn't ever
supposed to let anything bad happen to her ever again.

The front door didn't stand a chance and burst into a thousand pieces as Match flew directly through it. His enormous dragon body barely fit inside the great room and he wouldn't be able to get to his office at all in this form. He shifted once again this time in mid-flight and used the momentum to sprint to his personal sanctuary.

The door stood open and the blaze from the big fireplace lit up the hallway. Match could feel the heat coming from the room. It wasn't from the fire. Someone who had power over the element was in there. He could feel her magic reaching out and burning through his soul. Pain and pleasure, as it always was in his experience with love so far.

His dragon writhed inside of him, scales rippling across his skin. It pushed at him to rush into the room, take what was his, the one thing that had been denied to him for far too long.

The human part of his brain, the side of him that understood strategy and warfare, knew better than to do that. This situation called for strategy and being very careful in his approach. She'd tried to kill him one too many times in the past year, and the last thing he needed was to scare her into running away again.

Match slowed his breathing and straighten his spine. Could this truly be it? Was he finally going to be able to claim his mate?

The soul shard at his neck glowed with a passionate and hopeful light. This most prized possession had been given to him as a young man by a powerful witch who'd pulled a small piece of his soul from his chest and combined it with a sliver of the First Dragons soul. The magic inside gave him the power to shift from human to dragon, but more importantly, it showed him when he was in the presence of his true mate.

He should have given it to her long ago. The twinge of pain in his heart, right where she'd stabbed him, flared up to remind him, she might not want his soul shard, might not want him.

THE RED WITCH

*T*errible, horrible, no good, very bad.

She shouldn't be here. He was here and that was very, very bad.

Fallyn fingered the tip of the little dagger she kept up her sleeve and let its sharp edge pierce the skin just so she could feel its pain and know she was still alive. The small room she paced back and forth in felt far too familiar and yet she didn't remember ever being here before. The fire warmed her skin, the scent that filled the room made her heart beat faster, and she knew with all her heart that her end was near.

There was no other choice. She'd done everything else she could to ensure the Warriors were ready for the coming battle, the end of the world. Or the beginning of a new one. Maybe it was both. It was too hard to tell. Her mind couldn't hold onto the visions like it used to. She saw too much and not enough all at the same time.

She missed the voices in her head that used to tell her what to do, where to go, how to feel. They were all gone now, and her head was so silent. There was no way for her to know if she was making the right decision. It was her own fault they were all gone. She'd helped them fall into the arms of the enemy and now they'd all forsaken her.

What choice did she have but to come to the enemy himself?

If she didn't, the world would be taken over by darkness and everything she'd fought for would be for nothing. Besides, she was so damn tired of running and hiding. If she wanted that life, she should have stayed in Hell.

The necklace at her throat vibrated and Fallyn smacked her hand over it. She didn't like to think about the Mother, especially not to thank her for anything, but for this one gift, she was grateful. The pendant had warned her more than once of her enemy's approach and she'd used it to her best advantage. It took all of her will not to throw up the spell she used to hide.

The time for hiding was over. She had to face her worst fear... the great Red Dragon.

He was the final key to saving the world and restoring the balance between good and evil. He was also her greatest enemy. She'd tried to kill him more than once, but each time had hesitated at the last moment and only wounded him. She didn't like that weird tingly feeling in her chest that stopped her, but she supposed it was good that it had.

The final battle was coming sooner than anyone knew. It took her too long to understand that if the Red Dragon didn't come into his full power, the savior and the sacrifice couldn't happen. The Black Dragon and the Black Witch would win and spread death and destruction far outside the confines of Hell.

Fallyn gripped her dagger tighter in her hand. She couldn't

let that happen. She'd lived in Hell, grown up there, had the scars to prove it. Only the voices in her head, Izzy's especially had kept her from giving over to the evil. Those voices had never told her how big and wide the world above was. Probably so she wouldn't hope.

Not until the Winter Shadow and the Gold Witch had joined her in the underbelly of the caldera she thought was home, not until she'd faced her worst enemy as he found her for the first time and called her by her name, did she even realize there was life outside of pain and torture.

She used every part of her inner strength to escape and she wasn't going back. Yet, here she stood, waiting for Hell to suck her into its blackness. Because that's what it meant to be taken by a Dragon Warrior. She'd lost so many of the voices. At least her fath... no he wasn't her father. At least the Black Dragon couldn't get the voices now. The Black Witch couldn't use them for her revenge.

That didn't make sense and Fallyn shook her head to rattle the thoughts around in her brain. Without the voices, she had a much harder time understanding what her own mind was trying to tell her. Dragons meant Hell. She'd lost the voices to the Dragons. She'd had the voices in Hell, but they weren't there now. None of that made sense, yet all of it was true. Both were happening at the same time.

Unless she figured out where one particular voice hid, that of last mate, Hell, evil, darkness, revenge, would win. Everyone would be soulless like the Black Dragon. Dragons were the enemy.

She had one chance to turn the tide of the war. If she could convince the Red Dragon to call a truce, just long enough to find his mate, together, they could save the world. Surely that

was more important than hunting her down and destroying
her.

That's what he wanted, it was all he ever wanted. He'd
proven it time and time again. The last time they'd battle,
she'd had to save his stupid life. He couldn't die.

That too would destroy her.

Fallyn smacked her palm to her forehead and shook her
head. It was all very confusing. Where was Izzy to explain
things when Fallyn needed her most?

A red glow from the doorway caught Fallyn's eye and she
backed away. She reached for the fire and cupped a flame in
her hand, ready to defend herself from the attack. "I know
you're there, Dragon. Make one wrong move and I will cut
out your heart with a spoon."

The Red Dragon, in his human form, slowly entered the
room. He shoved his soul shard into his shirt, dimming it's
light. "A spoon? Wouldn't one of your daggers be more
appropriate?"

His hands were raised, his palms open to her, as if he
meant her no harm. Fallyn knew better. She crouched and
held the flame in her fist, ready to throw it in his face and
escape if she had to. "No. A spoon is dull and would hurt
much more."

"I see. What if I said you didn't need a dagger or a spoon?
That my heart is already yours."

Ah, she wasn't the only one who talked in riddles. That
made no sense at all. If she had his heart, they would both be
dead. "Don't try to trick me. I'm here to offer you a truce. Will
you hear me out or do we battle again?"

"Dammit, Fallyn. I'm not going to hurt you," he growled
low. His hands clenched into fists and scales rippled across his

SLAY ME   17

face. "I've waited a very long time to hear what you have to say."

So much anger and hate directed toward her had defenses she kept close at hand flaring up. She longed to throw every dagger she had at his face. Just looking at him made her sick. Her stomach fluttered, probably preparing to revolt. Her heart protested too, beating too fast, too hard. It always did in his presence.

That's how she knew to run. Not this time. "We have to find your mate, Red."

Shock and then a frown crossed his face. He didn't say anything, simply stared at her hard. Like she was crazy.

Pretty damn obvious he didn't like that idea. If he had any interest in finding his fated mate, the one that could help him stop the end of the world from coming, he would have been hunting for her all along. The other Dragon Warriors and even the wolves had been more than anxious to find their match. Poor daughters of dragons. So many had fallen and been lost to these bastards.

Not this asshole. That's what she got for trying to help a Warrior whose soul was already tainted by Hell. If they were lucky, he'd be mated to a Gold Witch, like the other Red. The light filled that Dragon's soul up so much, the darkness of the stain on his soul had burned away. But it had been a close thing.

They weren't lucky. Fallyn had seen the future, parts of it. This Red Dragon, master of fire, had to be mated to a Red Witch, mistress of fire. They were the final missing pieces to bring all the elements together. Only then could the balance be restored in the final battle.

Only then could she rest.

An interesting thought came to mind. "Is that why you've been hunting me?"

For a second she thought he was going to attack her. There was so much anger in his face. But also, other emotions she couldn't fathom. His shoulders sagged and he stepped closer.

Fallyn held out her dagger pointing it right at his heart. "That's close enough. Just answer the question. Have you been hunting me so I would find your mate for you?"

That would change her opinion of him, but only a little.

The Red Dragon took another step closer so that the tip of the dagger pressed against his chest. "You are my mate."

Fire burned behind Fallyn's eyes and hurt her brain. The necklace at her chest vibrated sending shockwaves through her skin and into her core. The room filled with a fiery red glow that she wanted to wrap herself up in and sleep for a thousand years. She was so tired, and everything hurt all the time.

She closed her eyes for just one second. In her mind's eye, she saw nothing but rivers of lava, black scaled beasts with beady red eyes, and the flames from the whip flying through the air toward her.

Dragons were the enemy. Fire was evil. Only the Black Dragon wielded fire with more skill than the damned Red Dragon. The sooner she found the enemy of her enemy his mate, the sooner she could finally be safe.

With her eyes still closed, she hissed out her words. "I see through your tricks. If you don't want my help, fine. I will go after your mate without you and bring her to you, lay her at your feet. I will not let your tainted soul lead us all into destruction."

"Fallyn."

Something about the way he said her name, changed the visions in her head. The darkness receded and turned to sunlight filtered through leaves. The scent of brimstone became ripe apples, and his voice became familiar.

That nice place burst into a thousand flames and she opened her eyes to stare up at the beast who'd betrayed her. She hadn't known that before now. She didn't know what he'd done to cause so much death and destruction, but she knew it was all his fault.

"Don't talk to me like that. Keep your lies to yourself. I can tell even if you say my name in that soft tone that feels like sunshine. Stay out of my head. Either come with me now to find your mate or suck it." She'd heard a woman say that to a man at the busy female filled place she wanted to take this Dragon Warrior to find his mate. It had worked well in that he then did exactly as the woman wished. The words felt clumsy coming out of her mouth, but they had an effect on him.

His eyes went wide and he took a step back. "Do you truly not know who I am? I thought... back in America when we fought against the Black Dragon and you saved me--"

Fallyn didn't like to think about that day. She'd had to make a deal with the Mother, and that meant she couldn't hide anymore. She clearly remembered asking her to save this Dragon, his head in her lap, tears streaming down her face. The rest was a fuzzy mess in her mind. "I saved you, because you have to find your mate and you stupid Dragons have to save the world and return the balance between light and dark. The final battle is coming."

Flames licked out of the Warrior's mouth. "I don't care

about any fucking battle. You told me to wait for you. You said not yet. If not now when?"

She wasn't afraid of his fire, only his lies and betrayals. "I never said any such thing to you. You're stalling and I don't like it. If you and the others don't defeat Ereshkigal, we are all doomed to live in Hell on Earth."

"I've been living that for the last two-hundred years."

He hadn't been living in Hell. She would have seen him there. The pain in his eyes said he knew what torture was. Just like her. Fallyn pointed her dagger at him again putting more space between them. She needed to get away from this Warrior. "Why are you trying to trick me. You cannot make me fall like the other women. I'm not made that way."

The hard, angry mask he wore slipped for a moment. "I can't imagine you falling for anyone if you didn't want to."

"Yeah. That's right and don't forget it." She had a feeling she was forgetting something important. "Now, are you coming with me to find your mate or do I have to find her myself and bring her back here to you?"

Some kind of emotion she didn't understand flashed across his face and he stepped back. "What did you have in mind for this mate hunt?"

Was he truly acquiescing? Hmm. It must have been the threat of bringing a woman back to his secret lair. "Come with me to a place I know that has a high population of human females. Since I cannot hear your mate's voice in my head, I believe that is the best chance we have of finding your her quickly."

The Warrior crossed his arms. "Where is this place with many women for seeking a mate?"

"There are many dotted around the globe, but there is a

small one near here in Bielsko-Biala. If we do not find you a mate there, we can go to several more in Krakow." She hoped his mate would be nearby, but she would drag him all over the world if needs be.

"If this is a place for females, how will I get in? I hope you don't intend to disguise me as a woman."

"There are men there as well, but more women congregate together." She had observed many such gatherings when she first emerged from Hell.

"Fine. Let's go now."

"These places are for humans and most are not open at night. We will have to go at first light."

"Tell me why the humans gather at these places. Maybe I know of them and can find one open now."

The only ones she'd found open in the evening were in the Middle East where the weather was so hot during the day, the people preferred to gather in the air conditioning and in the evenings. She'd discovered the human gatherings when she'd been spying on the Succubus Queen. The humans had these great buildings where they could find items to add to their hoards. Fallyn had been hard pressed to restrain herself from adding to her own collections, but luckily there weren't very many of the hoard stalls that carried what she coveted.

"No. I've done my research. Tomorrow we will go, and you will find your mate."

FEAR AND LOATHING IN POLAND

*H*oly Hell. She didn't know.

There were two other options, both of which Match hated. One, she did know they were mates and was being coerced by hell into tricking him for their own gain. That was very likely. On the other claw, she knew they were fated to be together and didn't want him.

All the old wounds from countless battles opened up inside of his chest, tearing at his heart. It was her right, her choice not to choose him. Even if fate decreed they were meant for each other, she could say no.

There would never be another for either of them. They would both live miserable existences until the end of days if she decided not to be his mate.

Not like it would be that much different than how he'd been living these past two-hundred and some odd years. Every day without her was worse than the next. Could she not feel that too?

She had been taken, presumed dead, so young, maybe she simply didn't know what would happen. It was unlikely Kur-

Jara or Ereshkigal had given her any glimpse of what a normal life would have been like for her. What their life could have been together.

Match's fire rose up, burning at the black stain on his soul, the mark all red dragons wore. It would be so easy to give in to the darkness and burn the world down, because that would take hell down too.

His memories of the day she was taken from him were wrapped in a well-guarded box with more locks than keys to open them and it was threatening to break open. He was the Red Dragon Wyvern, he couldn't afford to let anything distract him from his sworn duty to destroy every demon wyrm and their makers.

Memories were definitely a distraction. Especially the kind filled with fire, magic, and a loss worse than death.

If only he could give some of those memories to her.

Fallyn glanced toward the door like a caged dragon. "I don't like going out during the day, but the humans do, so we have no choice. I will return in the morning for you."

Not a fucking chance. He was never letting her out of his sight again. He'd only agreed to hear this insane plan to keep her here and talking to him. It was more than he'd ever hoped for and still it wasn't enough. He needed all of her. "No. You will stay in my home and rest. I'll have a room prepared for you."

"So you can trap me? I don't think so. I won't fall to your tricks like the other mates have." Her eyes darted around, looking for an exit route no doubt. Slowly, she moved away from him, but her back was already against the big stone fireplace. Fire and fear flashed in her eyes.

Shit. He hadn't meant to frighten her. He was never going

to convince her they were meant to be together if she stayed scared.

Never in his life had Match taken a submissive stance. The very thought of not being the biggest, baddest thing in the room grated on him and his dragon ruffled his scales. The alpha of alphas was always the most dominant man or beast in any room. Only for her would he stand a little less straight, turn his head to the side to expose his neck. For her he would kneel.

"I swear on my soul, you will come to no harm and you are not a prisoner. You can have full reign of any room as if this house was your own." In fact, it was. He'd built it for her, stone by stone, brick by brick. Even when he thought he'd never see her again. Now she was here, and he couldn't let her go.

The dagger she'd finally dropped to her side came back out and was once again directed at his heart. "Why should I trust you?"

She hadn't attacked him yet, maybe luck was on his side for just this one time. First Dragon help him find the right words to win her over. "You're the one who came to me. You want to strike a truce and work together. I kneel before you, Fallyn Ejderhanınkizi, and I swear my--"

He almost said self, but that wasn't what she wanted. Not yet.

"I swear my loyalty to your cause. Together we will find my mate and end the reign of terror brought upon us by the dark forces of Hell." Together they would find his mate, in her. If he had to move heaven, hell, and everywhere in between he would figure out how to help her recover her memories or defeat the foes forcing her to forgo mating with him.

He would go along with the farce of searching for a mate

to give him more time to convince her she was the only one for him.

Fallyn's jaw clenched and the fire banked in her eyes flared to life. If he didn't know better, he'd have thought she was about to smite him with dragon's fire. "You get up. You get up right now. I don't like this, you, in the position of weakness. You can't defeat Kur-Jara and Ereshkigal on your knees. Get. Up."

She held the dagger against his throat and pushed it against his skin until he had no choice but to get up. Even when he was at his full height, she pushed him even taller. Only when he had nowhere to go but on his toes or to shift into his dragon form to get his head any higher did she relent. "There. That's better. Don't do that again, warrior. I won't have it. You must be strong, the strongest. Do you hear me?"

"I hear you." He didn't understand her, but he heard the conviction in her words.

"Good. Then show me where you think I can rest. The sooner the sun rises, and we can hunt for your mate, the better."

He'd done something right, but he sure as shit didn't know what it was. She was confusing as... well, a woman. The other Wyverns were continually complaining about how they never understood their mate's minds and how confusing they were. Match had no experience with that part of the female anatomy.

He knew their bodies, but there was only ever one woman's mind he wanted to know. Now she was right in front of him and he had no idea what was going on inside her head. "Follow me."

As tough as she was, a frightened lamb in the woods

couldn't have been any more cautious. Her dagger remained in her hand and her stance ever at the ready to fight and draw blood. He wouldn't have anyone else startling her and risk losing her to the night. She knew well how to hide so that even the White Witch and the First Dragon weren't able to find her if she didn't want them to.

Warriors, clear the halls, take to your rooms. Give me and my guest some space. Few dragons were in residence at the moment, but the last thing he needed was one of his well-meaning nursemaids checking up on him or trying to help Fallyn. The only answer he received was the sound of several doors closing and flames being stoked in the fireplaces.

He led her to the south wing, where only he dared to go. This part of the house was off limits to everyone. Match's most prized possessions and the entrance to his personal hoard were hidden in these halls. He wouldn't take her there until he'd won her over. What he wanted to show her was much more precious than all the gold and jewels in the world.

"This part of the stronghold is my personal space. No others may enter, and it is completely secure. No one, beast of hell or human can get in without me knowing. You will be safe here." God, he hoped she liked it.

Fallyn raised one eyebrow and crossed her arms. She didn't say anything, but her expression screamed that she thought he was not the brightest spark in the fire.

He would show her. They entered through a stone archway and the big wooden door closed shut with a creak, a groan, and a bang. Fallyn jumped about a meter and pressed her body tight to his as a shield.

Oh.

Fuck.

He had absolutely no control over the reaction of his body, which was pumping an inordinate amount of lust into his every artery, vein, and organ at the moment because of her simple touch. One particular organ was receiving the brunt of the attention. Which was completely inappropriate. Even his soul shard was glowing, lighting up the hallway like a torch. Damn worthless thing.

Like he didn't know he was in the presence of his mate. He gritted his teeth and continued to walk forward, hating the space that put between them. He wanted nothing more than to press her up against the warm stone walls and kiss the crazy right out of her. Not yet. "You are safe, *biedronka*. I have sent everyone else away. No one will bother us in these rooms. They are for you and me alone."

"Then hurry up and get into the rooms." She shoved him toward the closest door, slipped into the bedroom behind him, and drew a symbol in the air. A shower of sparks dropped like a field over the entrance and he could no longer see anything in the hallway as if the door shut behind them. She moved around the room and drew the same sigil over the windows and even the fireplace until the room was basically glowing with the power of her spells.

This was how she hid from everyone. Including the White Witch and him. His gut said the magic was tainted by the darkness of evil from Ereshkigal. Showing off the bedroom he'd saved for their mating would have to wait. "That's a pretty fancy spell you got there. Where'd you learn it?"

"A mother. Not the mother, not the dark mother either." She paced back and forth in front of the fireplace.

Okay. That hadn't made a lick of sense. "Who taught you this magic?"

"She was a red witch, like me, like your mate. She was a mother and a mate, a sister and a soul mate. I'm not her. I'm not like her. She's like me."

Fallyn's babbling had that distinct bite of fear. Holy First Dragon. She wasn't just on edge, she was nervous. Not of the danger posed by their enemies, but of him.

Great. Just Great. This was not going like he'd thought.

If he was a hundred percent honest with himself, he'd hoped once he showed her the room he'd built for her, for them, that he could woo her and finally see the truth. That they were mates and he'd do anything for her. He'd waited hundreds of years lost and alone without her and now she was close enough he could touch, and she couldn't stand to be in the same room with him.

Okay. Okay. Shit. None of this was okay.

It's not like he didn't know this was going to be like flying against the currents, but he had hoped once they were finally alone together, secure in his lair, everything else would fall away. What a dumb douchcanoe he was.

Retreat now and live to fight another day. He fucking hated that strategy. He didn't back down from any fight. But dammit, it really was the right move. Maybe leaving her here in the marriage chamber filled with memories from their childhood would stir her own mind to remember who he was...who she was truly meant to be.

It would kill him to know she was under the same roof as he, only meters from his own room, and he still couldn't reach her. As much as he wanted her in his arms, in his bed, and in his soul, he would never fucking force himself on her. Not even if he thought that would break the spell Ereshkigal had on her.

"Then I take my leave of you, my lady. I'll be in the room adjacent should you need me." Match pushed his hand through the sparkling force field hoping it wouldn't hurt like hell and stepped through it into the hallway.

Right as he passed through the magical barrier, he heard Fallyn say, "I don't need you. You need your mate."

How true that was.

Match wanted to slam his fists into every stone and break the entire building down. Instead he deliberately took quiet steps to his own smaller bedroom and worked very hard not to splinter the door into a thousand pieces when she closed it. He stripped, careful not to shred his clothing, and threw himself down on the hard palette of his bed.

He preferred his bed firm, but not tonight. Tonight should be the softest of feathers with Fallyn's dark hair spread across his pillows. His face should be buried in her neck, reclaiming her as his. His cock should be buried deep inside of her, making her his mate, joining their souls as one.

His shaft thickened and became unbearably hard thinking about her lush body. She'd filled out since he'd first seen her in Hell.

He couldn't even imagine what she'd been fed. He'd feed her all the most decadent foods in the world if she'd let him.

He wrapped his hand around his cock imagining her lips sucking on a ripe juicy berry. He stroked, letting the pleasure take over, thinking of her licking the whipped cream from the top of an ice cream cone. But his fantasies quickly changed from a schoolboy's naughty thoughts of food to tasting Fallyn for himself.

Her hips were wider, and he longed to grab onto them and lick between her thighs. Her breasts were fuller and if he didn't get to see what her nipples tasted like soon, he would die. His hand sped up as he stroked himself toward climax.

He knew how to make a woman wet, had practiced exactly how to use his tongue to make her squirm and beg. He was well-versed in hearing his own name called out as a god as she came in his mouth or on his fingers. He could only imagine what it would feel like to push his cock into her wet welcoming heat.

Match bit down hard on his own lip to keep from calling her name as he came all over his hand. She was only one room away and still he couldn't have her. Jerking off to thoughts of her hadn't taken the edge off even a little bit. He shouldn't have even bothered. He wanted her more now than ever.

His own love, lost and now found, was within his reach, yet never farther from becoming his one true mate.

MEALS OF THE HEART

Fallyn was in the most luxurious room she'd ever seen in her entire life. She hated it.

Everything was closed in and she couldn't breathe. The only thing keeping her from busting right out through the window into the wild night was the familiarity of the stone walls. They were nothing like the pitted porous rock walls of her caves in Hell. These were hundreds of firm blocks carefully stacked in a repeating pattern that her eyes could trace from floor to ceiling, from window to wall.

She ran her fingers along the filled groove between each smooth square, until her lungs stopped working overtime and her heartbeat slowed. She could do this for hours. Maybe she had before. Before. Before what?

There were no more voices in her head to give her the answers to her never ending questions. The quiet scared her. If only Izzy could tell her every little thing was going to be alright. This room made her think someone else had told her not to worry about a thing once upon a time.

The scent of the Warrior lingered in the chamber, permeating everything. He smelled of fire and smoke like her brother and her father. Fallyn's back burned and she scratched her nails into the stone.

No. Not her brother. Jett had escaped Hell. He'd found a cure for his missing soul. Her name was Yvaine and someday she would be Queen. Or she would be dead, her blood stolen and used to make the evil more powerful.

Fallyn shook her head trying to rattle the right vision free. Which one was it? Both were happening at the same time in the future.

The outcome depended on her convincing the Red Warrior to find his mate. Which was practically impossible. She couldn't hear this damn stubborn mate. All the rest had been in her head, practically begging her to help them fall. She couldn't understand why they'd want to do that. The fallen did all sorts of strange things like kss, kss, kss.

At least she understood the biting. Biting was pain.

Pain was love.

She didn't understand love, but she knew pain.

Fallyn brought her hand up to the spot on her neck where she'd been bitten. The red dragon tattoo writhed under her fingertips, snapping its jaws and whipping its tail at her. Always so angry. Still, its presence brought her mind back to the here and now, but without that uncomfortable gnaw of fear.

Kur-Jara taught her the mark was the reason she was in Hell, and that by bringing her there he'd saved her from a worse fate. He'd wanted to kill the one who marked her so he could never get her, because a father always protected his daughters above all others. But that Warrior was protected by a very old curse. A curse as old as Kur-Jara himself. She should forget the warrior forever. He would never find her in Hell.

Her father had given her the gift of pain every year on her birthday so she would know what the Dragon Warriors were capable of, how a Warrior's fire could burn her just the same as Kur-Jara's fire whip. If she remained in Hell and helped him find the other mates, he could keep her safe, keep them all safe. He was wrong.

He was not her father.

She hadn't known about his lies until the first Dragon Warrior had come to Hell. He was cool like ocean water and his mate was a demon who smelled like nothing Fallyn had ever imagined before. She hadn't known about such delights as donuts back then. The delicious smelling demon mate had come to hell to find her Dragon Warrior.

Fallyn thought Jada should have left him there. She even tried to convince the demon mate of that, but the Red Dragon Warrior found her and attacked before she could. She only narrowly escaped him that time.

The angry mermaid tried to show her how the world outside of Hell was better, that Dragon Warriors weren't the bad guys. Fallyn never trusted Azynsa. She was destined to fall too and was hiding from the golden son. She made her Dragon Warrior come and get her in Hell.

Dragon Warriors could come to hell to find their mates. Kur-Jara had lied. So Fallyn left Hell. Izzy was happy that she did. After that the voices in her head got worse. The barrier of Hell couldn't muffle their cries and Fallyn heard them all.

Except this Red Warrior's mate.

Never her.

It wasn't the room Fallyn hated. It was the rush of memories being here that she didn't like. Nothing made sense and it all did. Battling her own mind exhausted her. Maybe she would rest. Just for a little while. She carefully took off her leather vest and leggings until she wore only her worn undergarments and threadbare t-shirt. The soft red was faded and dingy from being overly used.

Ninsy had tried to get her to wear other clothes she'd brought, or he'd brought. Or both. None had the protective element her leathers did. Only this red t-shirt with the glittering symbols had tempted her. The sparkle made her think of the hoard she'd left behind in Hell.

Fallyn crawled into the soft bed, but she wasn't used to such softness and she tossed and turned trying to get comfortable. When sleep finally came she dreamt of wolves and dragons, the moon and the sun, fire and blood. The same old dream faded and shifted into something else entirely.

Someone was feeding her a ripe, juicy strawberry. She'd never seen such a thing before and didn't understand how she knew what it was called. She did know the next delicious treat that floated into her mind. Ice cream. Ninsy had introduced her to it. This time the ice cream didn't feel cool on her tongue. Her whole body was overly warm, and a gnawing hunger grew in her stomach.

She woke with a start feeling aching and empty. Someone had cried out her name.

Her name sounded like pain.

That was enough rest for now. Fallyn threw the covers off, rubbed her eyes in the too bright light, rolled back out of bed and put her clothes back on. She was going to need some new ones soon. Her body had changed. She liked the new softness of her flesh. It was better than the sharp angles of her bones beneath her skin when she'd been in Hell.

She had every intention of putting more meat on her bones. That's what Ninsy had called it and squeezed her cheek. That thought made her stomach rumble, so she dressed and decided not to wait until the Warrior came back for her to go in search of food.

That idea immediately went to Hell. He was waiting for her in the hallway. Food would have to wait. "What do you want?"

His eyes went from her face, all the way down her body, and back up again. "You."

She felt like pulling out a dagger and poking his eyes out with it. He couldn't very well find his mate and save the world without those wandering eyes. "Me what?"

"You're the one who said we had to set out at daybreak to find my mate. I'm more than ready to find her, and it's morning. Thus, I am waiting for you."

Fallyn quickly glanced to the end of the hall where a window was set into the wall. Sunlight did indeed pour in. Huh. She'd slept through the night. That had never happened before.

"Fine. Show me which shadow portal will take us to the town." That would be the fastest way to get to the area where the human women would be waiting, and hopefully his mate.

"Oh no." He shook his head and growled. "We are not traveling by shadow. Ever. We'll fly. I can carry you."

He waved her out of the corridor and into the great room of his home. She followed him as far as the front door. She couldn't be sure he didn't have a whole fleet of dragons outside waiting to ruin everything. "Fly? So you can drop me into a lake or a pit to Hell. No."

Fire flashed in his eyes and scales rippled across his skin. "I would never drop you."

She'd angered him and the part of him that scared her the most was coming to the surface. "You're a dragon. I may as well let you eat me as soon as you shift into your dragon form."

"Oh, I want to eat you, alright." His words were low and husky. His dragon must be very close to bursting out.

"See." She was going to have to make a break for it. She backed toward the door and reached for her daggers. There was no way she was giving up on her mission now that she was so close to ending this war with Hell. "Get away from me. I'll go find your mate myself and bring her here. Give me your soul shard."

Another warrior walked into the room with his hands held up in the air. He had no weapons that she could see. Probably trying to lull her into thinking he wasn't dangerous. She recognized him. He was the mate of the Gold Witch. "Hi Fallyn, you remember me don't you. I'm Dax. I could just drive you guys. The Urus is right outside."

Fallyn pointed one dagger at each of the Warriors. "What's a Urus, and where is your mate? You're supposed to be protecting her."

"It's a Lamborghini SUV. Fire-breathing 4.0-liter turbocharged V8 under its hood with 641 horsepower and 627 pound-feet of torque, and Jules is with the kids at Cage and Azy's. She's fine. I promise." He smiled when he spoke of the Gold Witch.

The Red Warrior crossed his arms. "Daxton. I don't need your help."

"Of course not, boss. I just thought the lady might like to get on with her mission to save the world as soon as possible."

He knew. His witch must have convinced him. Good. One less enemy to battle. "Can your fire-breathing horse get us to Galeria Sfera quickly?"

"The mall?" Both warriors asked at the same time.

"If that is what you call the place where humans acquire things to add to their hoards. There are many women there and it is a good hunting ground for mates." She was a little surprised they knew of this place and had not scouted it for their mates before now. Dumb dragons.

"We are not going to the mall. I hate the mall. I don't even like shopping. What makes you think anyone could find a mate in a place like that? It smells like fried food and cleaning products."

"Dude. I could totally go for a burger at the American Restaurant." Dax licked his lips and rubbed his stomach.

"No. If Fallyn insists we go someplace with shopping and lots of humans, we'll go someplace not so claustrophobic like the Sukiennice in Kraków."

Aha. He did know where to find his mate. He'd been holding out on her. "Are women there?"

"Yes, of course."

"And food?" She was hungry and preferred not to waste time hunting for a meal.

The Red Warrior stepped closer and lowered his voice for only her to hear. "I'll feed you, Fallyn. You don't have to get something to eat at the market."

His words, the suggestion of him feeding her made her

stomach feel strange. Not hungry, at least not for food. She'd need to be wary of any sustenance he offered her. "How fast can we get there?"

He hesitated like he knew his answer wouldn't please her. What did he care about making her happy? He was her enemy and she would do well to remember this was a temporary truce. "A couple of hours drive."

She didn't like that answer one bit. He'd been right to worry. "No, we can be there in minutes by shadow."

Dax raised his hand. "If I'm driving, we can be there in less than an hour and we can grab some pierogis to eat on the way."

"What's a pierogi?" The word felt funny coming out of her mouth but seemed familiar.

"It's basically dough wrapped around meat or vegetables or both. They're delish and you're gonna love them. Come on. Let's go."

Before she knew it, they were all in a bright red vehicle, where Dax insisted she and the Red Warrior sit in the back seat together. He sped away much faster than she'd seen any dragon fly and it squished her up against the Warrior whenever they went around any corner. She was about to complain when they pulled up to a small roadside stand and she was handed a plate of tiny hot pillows of some kind of food with a dollop of cream on top. It smelled so good her stomach rumbled loudly, complaining that she hadn't eaten in far too long.

The warriors haggled for more amazing smelling foods and then they were once again on their way. Fine. She supposed if she had taken time to find food herself it would have been a wait equally as long anyway. She ate in silence and waited on high alert for any fishy business from either of the dragons.

This Urus thing was a handy contraption. She'd seen them of course but had never ridden in one. Still not as fast as traveling by shadow. Maybe these Dragon Warriors worried that the shadow would deepen the dark tainted curse on their souls. Maybe it would. Her own soul was as dark as they came with only the smallest spark of something old and bright inside.

"So, Fallyn, murdered anyone lately?" Dax looked at her in a small mirror.

She might steal that later. It could come in handy. "Only the soulless beasts surrounding the homes of unsuspecting Dragons and their witches."

"Dax." The Red Warrior growled the other one's name. He probably didn't like that his guard hadn't kept their land better protected.

"Just making polite conversation. We don't exactly know a whole lot about our red witchy guest. Except for the fact that she's your--"

The Red Warrior smacked Dax across the back of the head. "Not helping. Just keep your eyes on the road and get us to the city center fast."

She was the Red Warrior's what? Fallyn wanted to ask what Dax was going to say but didn't want a smack of her own. It would be harder to defend herself in such tight quarters. Although she was well practiced at it. The demon wyrms had learned long ago not to corner her.

"Here. I got this for you." The Red Warrior thrust something toward her.

A weapon? Their peace was over sooner than she'd hoped.

They hadn't even had time to look for his mate yet, much less find her. But when she glanced down at his outstretched hand there was no dagger or even a claw.

"It's szarlotka, apple cake. You used to... I mean, I think you'll like it." He had a look on his face that she did not understand. His eyes wanted something. Not in that covetous needy way Kur-Jara had. This was more like he wanted something for her instead of from her.

Weird.

She took the food from him and sniffed it. Warm, sweet apples, cinnamon and...

"Fallinka, Matchek, where are you? Come to the house now, it's time for the party."

"That's nanny. We'd better go," he grumbled and got up from where they were laying in the sun dappled grass. He reached for her hand, but she pulled him back down.

"Not yet, Match. I like it here in your lair. It's quiet." She hadn't told anyone that sometimes she could hear other voices in her head besides her own. But sitting in this cool shady copse of trees, holding Match's hand, the voices were quiet.

He ran his fingers over the tender spot on her neck where he'd bitten her. It tickled more than hurt. "I'll build you a house here made out of big stones. Then we can live there together. It will be as quiet as you please."

"Like a castle?" His family was very important. Her papa said so. If he said he could build her a castle, he could.

"Yes, like Tęczyn Castle. But better because we'll have apple trees in the back garden."

"What about mamma and papa? Can they live in the castle too?" Her mama was beautiful and fun. Her papa was big and strong. Somehow, she knew that someday Match would be bigger

and stronger. She could see him as a fierce warrior just the same as him being a sweet boy now.

"I'll build them a house too, but over there." He pointed back toward the village. "I want you for myself."

She liked that idea. Then they could run and play in their apple orchard and he could show her his dragon and she could show him her fire. Mama had said not to show anyone her fire, but fair was fair. He wasn't supposed to show her his dragon either.

If he was going to build her a castle, she wanted to make him something too. She wasn't big and strong like he was. But she was smart. Mama said that's why she could use the fire magic. "I made you something for your birthday."

He sat up straighter, excited. "What is it. Will you give it to me now?"

"No, silly. It's back at the house. I made you a szarlotka."

YOUR LOVE IS BETTER THAN
EXPLODING ICE CREAM

*M*atch was doing a damn shitty job of wooing Fallyn.

She'd taken the slice of apple cake, stared at it for a long time and then shoved it into her bag. It's not like he expected a thank you. He doubted Ereshkigal or The Black Dragon were big on manners. He had hoped a taste of her favorite childhood treat would help her to remember.

Maybe she did and remembering wasn't the problem. If that wasn't it, he was back to Hell coercing her to sabotage his fight against their evil plague. But not knowing which, he'd have to work both angles.

"We're almost to the old town square. I'll drop you two off and find someplace to park." They had made it to Kraków in record time. Match would maybe get himself one of these bigger vehicles. He didn't much like to drive, because flying was faster. But if Fallyn wouldn't fly with him, he could be almost content with the speed of the Lamborghini SUV.

"No, you'll valet the car so I can access it later and go about your other Wyr business. We don't need a chaperone." The sooner he could get Fallyn alone, the better.

Dax turned almost all the way around in his seat to look at him. "Uh, are you sure? Because she has almost ki--"

Fallyn threw her empty plate at him. "I'm not here to harm the Red Warrior. I'm here to help him find his mate, which he should have done already. I don't know why I have to do everything. You'd think you dragons wouldn't want the world to fall into darkness either."

"Jules says to trust you, so I'm going to. But if you kill my Wyvern, there will be no more pierogis for you," he shook the paper plate, "because you'll be dead. Got it?"

Why in the hell did everyone think he was some kind of giant baby who couldn't take care of himself. Yes, Fallyn had tried to kill him, but she hadn't. Each time they were together, he saw a new side to her. The last time, in the second battle at Rogue, she'd saved his life. "Don't threaten my ma-- guest."

Dax shrugged and grinned like he was fucking having fun. "Sorry, dude. That's my job. You gave it to me, so I'm gonna do it. Here we are. Door to town square service. I'll leave the car at the Bonerowski Palace hotel. Mostly because I like to say Bonerowski, but also you have an account there and they take care of the car."

Fallyn looked out the car window to the groups of people filling Krakow's town square. She sighed as if steeling herself to go out there. He could empathize. People were not really his thing.

"We don't have to do this. Search your heart, Fallyn. You know deep down that--"

She opened the car door, got out, and slammed it shut. Fine. She wasn't ready. He would play her game a bit longer.

He simply needed a little more time to figure out how to break through to her.

When he didn't immediately get out of the car, she motioned for him to hurry up with the cutest damn exasperated look on her face. She'd always been a sensual goddess to him, never cute.

He liked both.

Match got out and circled around the front of the car. Dax rolled the driver's side window down looking like the cool guy he was. His easy-going demeanor and his prowess in battle were half the reason Match had promoted him to Second Wyvern. They were opposites and yet still the same. "I want you to send out additional patrols. Having Fallyn here may also mean The Black Dragon and Ereshkigal are nearby. I will do my best to get the truth out of her. I expect you to protect our home."

"Good luck, boss. Don't get murdered." Dax saluted and sped off leaving Match standing in the street with nothing to do but follow his mate on a wild goose chase.

"Come, Red Warrior. I see many groups of potential mates for you. They are gathering at the big market building over there." She pointed to the big Cloth Hall where local handmade goods were on sale for tourists. He hadn't been in there since he was a young man. Maybe he would find a pretty amber necklace to buy for her.

Match's soul shard lit up underneath his shirt. He couldn't see it light, but he could feel its heat. The dragon part of him didn't like the idea of her wearing anything around her neck except for his soul shard. He would give it to her right now, if she'd take it.

"Fallyn, please, call me Maciej."

"No." She stepped away and her eyes flitted about like his fucking name scared her.

He lowered his voice and spoke softly, trying to soothe her with his tone. There were a lot of people around and having her pull out a sword or a dagger would cause a panic. "The humans will not want to be near us if you keep calling me the Red Warrior. They are already looking at us strangely. How about Match, can you call me that?"

"No. Your name tastes bitter in my mouth, or maybe in my mind."

He couldn't fix her mind, but he could give her something sweet. He sorely wished that was a kiss, but an ice cream would have to do. He ignored the tightening in his pants and searched the square for an ice cream shop. "Fine. Look over there, a group of women having a treat. Let me buy one for you and we can talk to them."

"Finally." She marched across the big plaza like a soldier on a mission.

Great. She was definitely going to scare these poor women. He hurried to catch up and put himself between Fallyn and the group of tourists. Americans if he was judging the accents right. Maybe Canadians? Hopefully. They were nicer and more understanding than most other visitors from abroad.

When they were within hearing distance, Fallyn shoved him toward the group. "Go. Kss, kss them and see if they light up your soul shard."

The women giggled. Great. One of them licked her cone all seductively like that was going to do anything for him. She was not his mate. "Is this some kind of dare or something. I'll kiss you, Mr. Hottie."

Her friend winked at him. "I'll do more than kiss you if you want. You're the first super hot guy we've met since we got here. I was starting to think Poland was going to suck and not in the fun way."

Match might hate having to stand here and talk to any other woman besides his mate, but his nanny would smack him upside the head if he forgot his manners. She might be gone these last hundred years, but her spirit would haunt him if he was an ass in front of company. "Welcome to our country, ladies."

The first woman squealed. "Oh my gawd. Your accent is so yummy. Say something else."

Before he could excuse himself from their flirtations, Fallyn came up to him, reached inside of his shirt and pulled out his soul shard. It sparkled in her hand and she glared at it like it was a piece of dung. "Talk to that one again. She may be your mate."

The women burst into more laughter. The one with the ice cream cone came over to them and got right up in his space, pushing Fallyn aside. His dragon stretched and fumed inside, not liking the way these females were treating his mate one bit. He'd love to shift and bite all their heads off then grab Fallyn up and fly her away.

It had been far too long since Kraków had seen a live dragon. It would be good for them.

"The translation may be a bit off, but the sentiment is just right." She held her ice cream cone right under his face and licked it from top to bottom, letting all kinds of drips dribble down her chin. "I'll mate with you, baby."

Smoke rose up from the sides of the cone and the top blew off right into the girl's face. She screamed and threw the now flaming empty cone on the ground. "What. The. Hell? I am so going to sue the bejeezus out of this ice cream shop. They think they can play pranks on poor unsuspecting tourists. I don't think so. I'm calling my lawyer."

Yep. Definitely Americans.

Match glanced at Fallyn who had a very suspicious smirk on her face. Had she lit the cone on fire?

Flames of his own whipped through his veins, the kind that burned for her. Jealousy was a very good step in the right direction. If he wasn't afraid for these desperate women's lives, he'd kiss one just to see what his Fallyn did.

"Please excuse us, ladies. We'll take our leave of you now and let you attend to your business." He turned, placed his hand in the small of Fallyn's back and guided her away from the ice cream shop.

"Don't touch me there. It makes me feel funny." She took a huge step away from him but did not stop or look back at the women she'd thought of as potential mates. "I don't understand why your shard lit up for them. Is it broken? None of them were your mates. They were too silly and stupid. You need a mate who is fierce to help you save the world."

Indeed, he did. "Someone like you?"

"Yes."

Match tripped over nothing. He'd need to tread very carefully, or he'd be falling on his face for her. "I'd like that. A mate... like you."

"Of course, you would. I would kill Kur-Jara here and now if he was here. But I will not be your mate. I will not fall for a Dragon." She shook her head at him and kept walking.

"Dragons are not your enemy, I'm not your enemy."

She wasn't listening and moved quickly into the crowds of

people. She was headed for the big Cloth Hall and if she slipped inside before he caught up to her, she could easily lose him and escape again forever. "Fallyn, wait."

She stopped dead in her tracks right at the entrance to the hall. Wow. She'd actually waited for him. Or not. She stood staring into one of the seller's stalls, clenching and unclenching her fists.

Match searched for the danger. Had a demon wyrm snuck in through the shadows of the darker corners of the building? He didn't smell any of the bastards. He didn't sense any danger at all. Only throngs of people and hundreds of vendors hawking their wares. He approached her slowly so as not to scare her and tried to figure out what she was staring at.

All he could see were hundreds of handmade Christmas ornaments. She'd stopped in front of the stall that perpetually sold decorations for the yuletide tree all year long. "Would you like me to buy you something here, *biedronka?*"

"No. I would like to kill this human and make him give me back all my things. I don't know how he found my hoard. It is very well hidden. But he has and it cannot be allowed to stand."

Aw, shit. There were a half dozen more Christmas shops just like this one. If it was sparkling things she was after, there were also at least ten jewelry vendors and who knew what else she'd decide was hers. Either there was going to be a murder spree, or he was about to go broke. "No need, love. Let me take care of this for you."

"I want to kill him." She was practically vibrating, and wisps of smoke floated up from her fingers.

"If you do, all the humans will run screaming. You don't want that, do you?"

Her gaze finally broke from the glittery baubles and she glanced around. "No. That would be bad, I guess. I will have to lure him away and kill him in the shadow."

A flame lit up in her eyes and the time for negotiations and calm was over. Match reached into his jacket and pulled out his wallet. "How much for everything?"

The shop vendor smirked. He was messing with his own life.

Match switched to Polish and pulled out his Black American express card to show he wasn't joking around. "*Jak bardzo? Pospiesz się i powiedz mi.*"

"Whoa. *Jedną chwilę, proszę.* Umm, let me do a few calculations." His eyes went wide and he fumbled for his phone, quickly recovering and tapping away.

Fallyn poked him in the back. "They are mine."

"I know. I'm getting them back for you. Then you can do whatever you wish with them. This human will never bother you or your things again. I swear it."

"Don't make promises you can't keep."

"I will do my best not to, but this one I can keep." He turned back to the shop owner. "I estimate your inventory is worth no more than say fifty-thousand złoty. Please charge that to my card. One of my people will contact you later today. I'd like you to come work for me acquiring these kinds of trinkets for my... friend. Whatever you make here in the Cloth Hall I will double."

"Seriously? Okay, yeah. I see you're being very serious. That, that sounds fine. Thank you, sir." The man took Match's card and had to run it through the credit card machine five times to charge the full amount. He was already lamenting the call he'd get from his accountant later. "Do you want me to box it all up and ship it somewhere?"

"Fallyn, where would you like the nice man to send your Christmas ornaments." He couldn't imagine she had a home with a mailing address. But any information he could get about where she went to hide from him would be more than he had now.

"I will take them with me." She reached for a large glass bulb painted with a wintery Polish landscape scene. She stared into the thing just like she had at that damn szarlotka.

"Call this number and they'll tell you where to ship the rest. Then, please close up your shop. You'll hear from my people soon about your new position." He handed the man a card with Dax's contact information. Match was not a logistics kind of guy. That's what his second was for.

Now to get Fallyn out of the hall before she discovered any other vendors with shiny sparkling objects she coveted. Now that he knew what she liked, he would choose several items from his own hoard to give to her. Maybe she would like some dangling bobs for her ears. He had a pair of fifteenth century Byzantine earrings with very rare and precious red diamonds that he would like to see sparkle in the light of the flames in his favorite fireplace as they made love.

Longing hit him so deep in the gut that he was sure his entire chest was one big empty hole.

"Warrior. What is the matter? Do you sense the coming danger? Warrior?"

He needed a minute and stared across the plaza just to avoid staring at her beauty. Maybe this facade of searching for his mate with her wasn't such a good idea. The longer they spent together, the harder he felt the absence of their connec-

tion in his soul. Something had to change, or he wasn't going
to get anywhere with her and that was unacceptable.

They'd done it her way. Now it was time for his way.

"Fallyn. Call me Match.

She scowled at him and reached for a dagger but looked
around at the people pushing past them. The square was
getting busier by the moment.

"Say it or I'm not searching for a mate, I'm not flirting with
other women, and I'm not taking another step until I hear my
name come out of your mouth." The fires banked inside of
him for so long flickered and sparked to life. This woman was
his and it was his job to protect her, keep her healthy and
happy, and to make sure she knew that she was loved.

She was fiery and ferocious and furious with him. Her
determination to defeat the darkness and make the world
right despite the horrible life she'd been dealt made her all the
more amazing. Even if he'd never seen her before today,
hadn't known since childhood that she was his one true love,
his fated mate, he would still have fallen so hard for her that
any other women in his life would be erased.

Good thing there had never been any other women.

There was only her and her goddamned determination to
drive him insane.

With her newfound reticence to draw her weapons among
the humans, Match pushed his luck and moved into her
personal space. "Say my name, Fallyn."

And be mine again.

Steam evaporated from her skin and the sparkling head of
a red dragon tattoo poked its way out from under the collar of
her shirt. He couldn't help but reach for it. The design was
childish and unfinished, but it was still his mark. The moment

his fingertips touched her skin his soul shard lit up like a bonfire on a moonless summer night.

The softest of whimpers escaped her mouth. "Match."

That was all it took. The walls he'd built around his heart crumbled and he could hold back no longer. He pulled her into his arms and took her mouth in a kiss that had been waiting for a lifetime.

NOT MY DRAGON

*F*allyn was going to kill Match.

Just as soon as she figured out where her knees had gone to and her brain came back from the lovely soft fuzzy place it basked in at the moment.

She understood now why the witches all did this strange lip pressing thing with their dragons. It felt incredible. Like her whole body was standing on top of a mountain singing while wrapped in a warm blanket. She wanted to laugh, she wanted to cry. She wanted his tongue to dance with hers some more.

"This is why she fell for him."

A new voice in her head said that. One she didn't remember hearing before, but it was so familiar. She tried to respond, to draw the voice in and find out who it belonged to. The voice had to be his mate.

Yes. The new voice said she fell for him. For Match.

Oh. Then this mysterious new mate's voice was the one who should be kss, kss, kssing him now. Not her. Fallyn could ruin everything. This wasn't her mate. This wasn't her dragon.

She didn't have a dragon. She didn't have a mate.

"Yes, she did."

Ack. The voice. She did what? Ruined their last chance to save the world?

Fallyn shoved Match hard and then slugged him in the mouth being careful not to let her new treasure get broken. Like her heart. "Don't wreck everything."

She waited for his retaliation but all he did was rub his jaw where she'd hit him. "That was the very opposite, love. That kiss was the most right thing that's happened to either of us in a century and a half."

"No. Don't you do that again. Your mate is near. I heard her. We will hunt for her now and with no more distractions."

Scales rippled across his skin and the fire in his eye flickered and flamed. Now she'd done it. She'd awakened the dragon within. Should she run and hide or stay and fight? She didn't even know if she'd be fighting for her life or the lives of everyone else around them.

He thought she was dangerous around humans. But he was the one who could end them all with one swipe of his tail, one breath of his fire, one kiss from his lips.

"One kiss. More kisses. My kisses. They're mine. He's mine."

He raised his arms into the air as if they were his great wings, but he didn't shift. He spun in a circle and shouted. "Where, Fallyn? Where should we hunt for this enigmatic mate of mine? Huh? Don't you think if she were this close to home, I would have found her by now? Do you think me a complete fool?"

Smoke was starting to come out of his ears and his pupils elongated into that of his beast. He stalked toward her, but she stood her ground. He was mad. Well, dammit all to hell, she was too. She'd given up everything for him.

He stood toe to toe with her, towering over her, trying to intimidate her into submission. She submitted to no one. He could tell too. Still he continued to rage.

"Do you think I have not searched heaven and hell for my mate? She's been within my grasp for years and I never even knew. She hides from me, she reviles me, and still I love her. I have been ever faithful to her and only her. You want me to find her, mark her, claim her, and mate her. I want that more than anything else in the world."

The way he looked at her, the passion of his plea, recommitted Fallyn to this mission. His mate wanted him. She wanted to fall. He wanted her to fall for him. Everything would be right in the world when that happened. To quiet his angry beast, she spoke softly. "Then we will find her, and she will be yours."

The muscles in his jaw ticked and he searched her eyes, maybe deeper into her soul. No one had ever looked at her this way. It took him a long time to find whatever he was looking for inside of her. But he finally did and the dragon in his face faded and the powerful man returned.

He nodded and stepped back. "Then lead the way."

She'd won this battle with him. So why did it feel like she'd lost?

Fallyn glanced around the square while Match watched her. He was right. This was not where he'd find his mate. There were too many people here and the outside voices drowned out the soft new voice in her head. They needed to go somewhere quieter.

When Dax had driven them into the city, she noticed a

green area with trees and far fewer people circling this old part of the town. "I don't know if your mate is this way, but will you come with me to a place away from all the noise? Maybe I will be able to hear her better there."

"Where you go, I go." He held out his hand indicating that she should go first.

They went down a side street off the side of the square and at this point, Fallyn was simply following her nose. She smelled earth and greenery, but also roast chicken. Her stomach rumbled loud enough that Match heard.

He laughed. She didn't think it was very funny. There were many days in Hell where her stomach became so empty it forgot how to rumble.

"Even while saving the world, we have to eat, love. Hold on a moment and I'll get us some food." He stepped into the shop, handed a young man near the entrance a wad of paper and came back to join her on the sidewalk. Before she could even ask where the food was, the young man trotted out with a paper bag that smelled of more than just chicken. Match took the bag and handed over more paper.

This paper must be something humans liked to hoard because it made the young man very happy. She did not care for it. While it had colorful designs on it, there was no shine or sparkle like her glass bulb or her daggers.

"Come on, we'll have a picnic in Planty Park then walk down to the river. Maybe we'll find my mate there." He led her to exactly the green grassy area she'd been thinking of and already the world was quieter.

"It's not likely your mate will be near the river. She is a fire witch, not a water witch." She was sure she'd already told him that. A fire witch for a fire dragon.

Fallyn had fire. Did she have a fire dragon too?

No.

"Yes."

Match found a spot for them to sit under a tree where sunshine dappled the ground. They sat and he pulled out the food, allowing her to choose what she wanted first. "I knew that."

"You did?" She found it surprisingly nice sitting here with him. Like they'd done this together before. No battles, no evil, just food and something else she didn't understand. A feeling from inside that wasn't fear, or anger, or sadness, or even pain.

"Hmm, yes." He slid another piece of apple cake toward her. "There are many things I know about her. Like the fact that she likes szarlotka, shiny baubles, and has a heart of gold."

"Gold? No wonder she is so precious to you. You will not melt her heart and keep the gold for yourself, will you?" Who knew what a covetous Dragon would do? Even the mere scent of gold had sent Kur-Jara crazy. Almost as crazy as when he found a mate or a soul shard that he could steal. But soul shards could only be given, not taken.

"I do hope her heart will melt for me, but only she can give it to me. I cannot take it. Trust me, I've tried."

Hearts must be like soul shards. She hadn't known that. "Then we must hurry and find her, so she can give you her heart and you can give her your soul shard. Only then can the sacrifice and the savior defeat Ereshkigal and her curse."

"Where did you learn about this sacrifice and savior?" The way he asked the question sounded like he didn't care and was just talking to talk. But his body was on alert and she knew her answer mattered to him very much.

"I think I've always known. I don't remember a time when I didn't."

His muscles in his shoulders tensed and he set his food down. "I do."

She didn't understand. Match talked to her differently than anyone else she'd ever known. Even the mates who'd come down to hell got frustrated that they couldn't understand her. She saw too much, heard too much and didn't really understand the difference between what was real and what was to come. Both were true.

Ninsy had tried to help her practice, but as the Mother's priestess, she couldn't be trusted. No one could.

Fallyn had used up so much of her energy finding the mates, putting the sacrifices and saviors together and she'd been tired for a while. Right now, when she'd had a good night sleep and more food in a day than she could remember, she was exhausted.

"Why can you remember something I can't?"

"A Dragon's memory is very long and we never forget." He picked up the apple cake she was afraid to eat and stood up. "Come on. I want to show you something."

They threw the paper bag and food wrappers in the trash and slowly walked down the wide path through the green grassy area in the busy town. Soon enough a castle came into view. But it was the wrong castle.

"Who lives in that castle?"

"No one now. But long ago a King called Krakus lived there."

"How long ago?"

"Before either you or I was born. King Krakus was ruler in the time when the sons of the First Dragon roamed free throughout the land."

"Was the king afraid of the dragon?"

"No. He was friends with him."

Hmm. She wasn't sure she believed Match, but she wanted him to continue the story, so she kept quiet about it. She had a feeling someone was going to die at the end. "I see. Go on."

Match continued to lead her along the path toward the castle and she could smell the river. The dragon in the story must have been a blue one.

"The king had a daughter who was very beautiful and very special. She could control the element of fire."

Just like her. "Did she have to live in Hell, or did she hide?"

"Neither. She fell in love with the Dragon."

Fallyn gasped. She did not see that coming. Now she knew for sure someone was going to die. "Did the dragon eat her?"

Match choked and had to look away. Probably because he didn't want to tell her. She understood, he was trying to show her that not all Dragon Warriors were bad. He wasn't.

She'd been wrong about him.

"The Dragon fell in love with her too."

A man walking with a small beast that resembled a wolf, but much smaller almost collided into her as he passed them. She'd been paying too much attention to Match and his story and not enough to her surroundings. Dumb mistake that she would not let happen again. She side-stepped to avoid him and instead bumped into Match's big muscled arm.

He grabbed her hand to keep her from careening to the ground and even when the man and his beast were far from them, he continued to hold her hand. He was a keen warrior. Perhaps he sensed danger and didn't want to alarm her.

It wasn't like she couldn't defend herself. She'd been doing that for years. But it was sort of nice to think someone else in the big world might look out for her. She would return the favor and gripped his hand slightly tighter so he would know she had his back too.

"What happened to the dragon and the daughter?" She bet the mother turned this woman into a dragon daughter. He was probably telling her this story to prove that he remembered many things from long ago, including the first dragon daughter.

"The dragon had a brother who always wanted what his twin possessed."

Uh-oh. She didn't like this story anymore.

"The brother's fought over who would mate the princess and they tore the castle and the city surrounding apart. The villagers were scared, and they asked the king and his sons to put an end to the dragon's fighting. He offered a reward to any man who could find a way to stop the dragons from destroying everything."

"The reward must have been very valuable for a human to come between fighting dragons."

"He offered his daughter's hand in marriage."

"But she..., no, I don't like it. That's not right. He must have offered piles of gold or jewels or something else. You are wrong. You're telling the story wrong."

"Don't get mad, *biedronka*. We can't change the past."

"Well, the king is stupid, and I hate him."

"I don't like him much either. But he did offer his daughter's hand in marriage and many men tried to stop the dragons. Too many died."

See. She knew someone was going to die.

"The daughter did not like this battle or the fact that she

was supposed to be the reward for stopping it. She decided she was going to do something about it. She dressed herself up as a young man and called herself Skuba. She went to the King with a plan. The only time the dragons stopped fighting was to eat so she would to trick them into eating something so vile they would have to rush to the river to drink away the taste. She prepared two roast lambs and filled one with the fire of her love and the other with the bitter sulfur of unrequited love."

"I like that the daughter took charge. No man should get to give away his child like that. He should have protected her from the dragons."

"Don't worry, I promise the story has a happy ending. Do you want to hear the rest?"

She wasn't so sure. "Fine. Keep telling it."

"The dragons did stop their battle to rest and eat and when they did, they found the lambs. The daughter had chosen one lamb that was slightly larger than the other knowing the covetous brother would go after it first, which of course he did. The sulfuric fire burned him all the way down to his soul and though he slunk away defeated to the river to drink. His thirst was never quenched. He knew he was defeated that day, not by his brother, but by the daughter's love."

"What happened to the dragon and the daughter who were in love?"

"The dragon's mother gave the daughter a ring made of fire to prove to all that she was the mate of the First Red Dragon Son. But his mother wanted to make sure a battle like this never happened between her children ever again. She took a piece of the love she had with the First Dragon and combined it with a small shard of each of her son's souls."

She knew the end of this story. She wasn't sure it was a happy ending as he promised. "And those shards glow when the dragon is in the presence of their true mate."

Match stopped their walk at a spot near the river, where the fortress wall of the castle stood tall against the sky. Red light sparkled in the evening light of dusk. Match's soul shard was glowing bright. "Without fail."

Fallyn's own necklace shivered against her chest. Danger was coming. "Your mate must be near."

The words brought dread that sank like a rock in the dark river water. She didn't want his mate to come and take him away. Away from her.

"She is. Very near. She just has to charge like the King's daughter did. She has to fight for me too, he had to open her heart to find me."

"Take charge."

Stupid. He wasn't hers. She didn't have a dragon. She didn't have a mate. Her necklace buzzed and Fallyn reached for her daggers. "There was one dragon who never got the gift from the mother, isn't there?"

"Yes." Match turned her to see a great metal dragon raring his claws and head up into the air. "The twin who lost the battle for the daughter's love refused his mother's gift and over time his heart turned black."

"Did he then go willingly to Hell?"

"No. Even with a black heart, there was still good in him. He was a Dragon Warrior after all and the son of the First Dragon. When the first great battle with Hell came, he was lost to the underworld forever. His brother tried to save him and failed. Because of that failure, all Red Dragon Warriors wear a stain of darkness on our own souls inherited down through the ages from the First Son."

The metal dragon hissed, and flame shot from its mouth. People standing around them on the sidewalk cheered and clapped their hands. Fallyn cried.

Cried for the dragon who couldn't love and whose heart turned black.

Cried for her own heart, because surely it must be black too.

Cried, because she wanted to love.

"Love Match."

LOVE AND LIES

The black stain on Match's heart scrabbled and scratched making sure the dragon didn't forget it was always there waiting to turn him into a dark beast with no remorse. Knowing that he would never have a true mate, Match had allowed the darkness to grow inside of him.

The day he'd gotten his soul shard, the very day he and Fallyn had claimed and marked each other, was the best and worst day of his life.

He'd felt so powerful and yet couldn't save her.

For so long he'd thought she'd died in that battle. She'd suffered a fate worse than death. Taken by Ereshkigal and the Black Dragon as a child and raised in Hell.

He should have saved her.

Now she was here in his arms, and he still couldn't save her.

His dragon fumed and raged. It wanted her love and to love her in return. It wanted to mark her again, reclaim her, and mate her. But even the animalistic part of him understood that her love could only be given. It would wait, not so patiently, but it would wait and continue to push his human side to win her over.

He'd hoped by showing her the Wawel Dragon and telling her the closely guarded secret of the First Red Dragon Son's failure that she might see what denying love meant and open her heart to him.

It was a stupid idea, because now she was crying. What the hell was he supposed to do with that? He didn't want to make her cry. He didn't even know she could. He could handle her anger, even her fear. He'd defend himself in a fight against her all day, every day, twice on Sundays if slashing him to ribbons with her daggers would make her feel better.

But he couldn't take her tears. "Fallyn, my love. Please don't cry. I'm sorry, I shouldn't have told you that story. I'd take it back if I could. Please, *biedronka.*"

First Dragon help him make this better.

"I thought you'd never ask." A tall, muscular man, with a prosthetic arm appeared next to them and stared up at the Wawel Dragon statue. "She's a tough one though, because I'm not sure my usual advice of lots of orgasms is the right answer for your little ladybug. Maybe just start with a lot more kissing. Work your way up to the orgasms."

A stunning woman with dark olive skin, curves for miles, and a flowing white dress joined the man and took his arm. They looked the picture of a happy, loving couple, who could also go to war and save the world at the same time.

Fallyn gasped and gripped Match's hand tighter, but she didn't move. Did she recognize these people? He didn't but felt like he should.

The woman smiled at them both and Match was sure he

knew her. Maybe she was a famous movie star or something. He wasn't good at keeping up with that kind of stuff.

"Hello, Fallyn dear." Her voice was soft and alluring. Like his mother's. "Don't be too surprised we're here. I did tell you when you asked me to save your dragon that you wouldn't be able to hide anymore."

Fallyn moved closer to him until their sides were pressed together. He would do the best he could to lend her his strength. It seemed to be the only thing he could do. Words wouldn't come out of his mouth and his muscles wouldn't move. Except to hold her hand. Fallyn seemed to have total control of herself though. She shook her head at the couple. "I never asked any such thing. I don't have a dragon."

"Hmm." The woman tapped her finger against her lips. "That was a pretty crazy day, what with the babies growing up so fast and the battle for their souls and all. That was a neat trick you did giving them some of your fire to start that growth spurt. But I do distinctly remember saving a first son at your request."

The man slugged Match in the arm. "You're looking good, kid. Back to fighting form. You're gonna need all your strength and battle prowess pretty soon."

That didn't sound ominous, no, not at all. But with Fallyn by his side, he could defeat death itself. He would take the man's advice and kiss her again and again as soon as he could move.

The warrior turned back to his lady love. "Hurry this along dear, we don't have much time."

The woman wiped away Fallyn's tears and looked into her eyes. "There's nothing more I can do. I cleared your mind of my sister's black magic that day too. But you recognized him even before that. You're the one keeping your heart in the dark. I know you've been through a lot and I'm terribly sorry we lost you for so long. But it's safe now and you need to listen to the voice telling you what you want."

More tears tracked over the woman's thumbs as she cupped Fallyn's cheeks. He'd asked for the First Dragon's help in making her stop crying, not bring more. Fallyn sniffled and touched her forehead. "But Izzy is born again. She's not in my head anymore. All the fallen are gone. It's so quiet now."

Match wanted to be the one to wipe away his mate's tears. He would take care of her forever if she'd let him. The words this goddess-like woman was saying to Fallyn were making a difference, he knew it all the way to his very core. Even his dragon was at peace with them talking to his mate and touching her. But when they were done talking, he was whisking his mate away and making sure she never cried again.

The woman touched the same spot on Fallyn's head. "But there's a new voice, isn't there? One you've been ignoring for a long time."

Fallyn's eyes went wide. "Yes. It's the Red Warrior's mate. I'm trying to find her for him, but it's hard. She's not very helpful and to be honest, neither is he. Why is she being so difficult. Can't you tell her to come out? I know you've helped the others. She has to help him save the world."

"Ah, you see, she's scared. She promised her heart to him long ago, but then she was taken away to a very bad place and taught that she was wrong to do that. But she wasn't. The ones who taught her that love is pain were wrong."

His poor brave Fallyn. If she would let him love her, he'd never hurt her.

"They lied to her." Fire licked through his mate's eyes. He shared her anger and would use his own fire to make sure the bastards could never lie to her or hurt her as long as they both shall live.

"Not exactly." The goddess shrugged and her eyes went all sad. "They've only found pain when they were looking for love. I was like that once too. I was jealous of what my sister had and wanted it for myself. I caused a lot of pain and suffering before I opened my heart to this big ole sweetie and he taught me what love truly is."

"You were wrong, but I thought the bad people who were mean to the Red Warrior's mate were wrong? It can't be both." Fallyn looked to him for confirmation, but he didn't have an answer for her. He wanted those that did wrong to be punished, especially if they wronged his mate.

But that would mean he would have to punish himself, because he'd wronged her when he let her be stolen away. He'd wronged her when he didn't use his entire life to search for her after the battle on the day he received his soul shard. The only thing he hadn't done wrong was loving her.

"Nobody is perfect, dear, and the world is not as black and white as you'd like it to be. I was wrong and I've worked for a very long time to try and set things right. But I haven't done a very good job. I made a lot of mistakes and I've hurt people." The goddess released Fallyn and rejoined her mate, taking his hand again. "I hope his dragon sons and my daughters of dragons can do better."

"They're going to save the world. I've seen it. They're also all going to die. I've seen that too."

Crap on Kraków. He knew she had some psychic abilities,

but to see all their deaths? He'd be scared shitless too. He was an ass for trying to push her so hard. That was the only way he knew - never stop in pursuit of destroying the plague of demon dragons, the Black Dragon, and the Black Witch, Queen of hell.

His dragon agreed. It wanted out, it wanted to fight and burn their enemies to the ground. That's what he'd done his entire life. Until he found Fallyn in Hell. Even then he used his mantle of hatred and anger for the evil to fuel his pursuit of her.

Look how that had turned out. She'd had to come to him, in truce. He may have never caught up to her if he kept fighting fire with fire. Only when he quieted his temper and rage had she truly responded to him. He wasn't sure he knew how to both burn for her and keep her from getting burned by him at the same time.

"Love of my life, we have to go. Jara is coming, now that he's found our Red Warrior again, he won't relent." The man pointed to Match. "You've got to give her your soul pretty damn quick here, kid."

"She doesn't want it." Finally, his mouth at least worked again.

"Sure she does. Just keeping trying. A dozen kisses a day, or an hour, should do the trick. But, son, I am telling you. Once you discover the joy of making love to your mate, I promise you'll be able to keep her happy with a dozen orgasms a day. Try using your dragon tongue to--"

A stream of fiery spittle flew past Match's face, narrowly missing both him and Fallyn. People screamed and ran in every direction away from the Wawel Dragon statue. Probably because there was a great Black Dragon perched on top of it, wings spread wide, creating a shadow big enough for the armies of hell to pour forth.

Dragon Warrior that he was, he ran toward the Black Dragon. "Fallyn, protect these people and get them to safety while I--"

A dagger whizzed through the air toward him followed by three more in rapid succession. He had to use his dragon's fast reflexes to duck so they didn't strike him down. Fuck. Why was she throwing her weapons at him? Had she been luring him to this battle all along?

He didn't want to believe that, but her body was a light with fire, and she had a sword brandished. She let out an unholy battle cry and ran straight for him. "Shift, you dumb dragon before they steal your soul shard."

Her sword struck home, not in his chest, but right through the stomach of a demon wyrm, pouncing on him from behind his left shoulder. Fallyn's daggers lay in a circle around him, each in the oily remains of dead wyrms. She'd just saved his life.

Again.

He shifted into his dragon form and laid a huge swath of fire in a circle all the way around the Wawel Dragon. That would keep the humans out and the demon wyrms in. They were from Hell, but a Red Dragon's fire was imbued with the White Witch's magic. Nothing dark survived its pure burn.

Thank you for saving me, love. He wanted to protect her, but she was no fragile ladybug. If they were to win this fight, it would be side by side. *Let's kick his ass back to Hell together.*

Fallyn whooped again and went ninja on those demon wyrms asses. They fell like mosquitos to a flame thrower, even though she hadn't even brought out her power over the fire. In fact, he didn't remember her ever using her fire to attack anyone or anything. Except maybe that ice cream cone.

Hey, Fallyn, my love. I think those demon wyrms trying to sneak through the wall of flames remind me of the woman at the ice cream shop. Don't you think?

Fallyn whipped around toward the wyrms he indicated and the whole lot of them burst into flames and their heads exploded.

"No, they do not remind you of that woman. You should never think of her again. Now stop screwing around and find a way to stem the flow of these beasts from Hell."

Match's normal battle rage should be flowing through him right now and instead he found himself laughing. The God-damned Black Dragon was about to breathe down his neck and he couldn't be more joyful.

She loved him. She just didn't know it yet.

Match spread his wings just as wide as the Black Dragon and sent a call out to his brethren letting his alpha voice ring strong. *Brother Dragon Warriors heed my call. Our enemy has shown himself among the humans we have vowed to protect. Come to me and together we will send him back to Hell where he belongs.*

The Black Dragon screeched and blew a plume of fire up into the air. *Oh, little brother. This is not my day to return to Hell. I've only just returned. It's been far too long since I visited the land of my youth. I've got castles to burn down and descendants of a King and his daughter to murder. Although I do appreciate the statue they erected to me.*

Today they sent him back to Hell, but next time they would end him and his reign of terror. Match had battled the Black Dragon before. He knew the bastard's arrogance. It would be his undoing.

While his enemy pontificated on his plans, allowing his minions to wreak havoc on the land, Match took the opportunity to send a fast super-heated blast of flame at the metal statue the Black Dragon grasped in his claws. The metal twisted and melted, wrapping itself around his scaly feet.

He'd have to donate a chunk of money to the restoration of the statue when this was all over. He'd always been kind of fond of it. Ooh. They could put out a news story that this was all a big publicity stunt to raise funds for the city's art installations. Smart.

The Black Dragon roared and flapped his wings to get away from the molten metal spiced up with Red Dragon fire. Match was sure it hurt like Hell. If they were lucky, he'd be a giant baby and run away to nurse his wounds.

"Match, look out, incoming." Fallyn shouted at him and he took evasive maneuvers. A stream of water spouted from the river, narrowly missing him and sent clouds of steam up around the Black Dragon. The melted metal twisted around the beast's legs, trapping him in mid-lift off. Excellent. They may be able to defeat this ancient foe today, here and now.

Match fucking hated river water. But he knew who loved it. *Hello brother. Please ask your lovely mate, Azynsa, to try not to put out my fire until after we defeat our enemy.*

Cage flew in through the steam clouds and hit the Black Dragon with rays from the sun so bright, Match was going to be seeing spots for a week. *I'm just sad she missed on her first shot. I thought she was aiming for your head.*

"Hey, I don't miss. If you two can't play nice, Fallyn and I are more than happy to take this asshole out on our own." From the bank of the river, a wave of water lifted a golden scaled dark-skinned mermaid up above the banks and gently deposited her on the walkway. She shot fountains of water from her hands melting demon wyrms almost as fast as Fallyn burned them to ashes.

The Black Dragon roared and screeched and flapped his wings, trying to get free from the metal. More demon wyrms popped up out of the shadows of the trees and the castle wall. *Kill him and get his shard, my sons.*

Well, fuck. Match shouldn't be surprised the Black Dragon was after his soul shard now. He'd made a play for all the other Wyverns'. *My soul shard does you no good if I'm dead, Kur-Jara.*

From the tunnel leading to the Dragon's Lair beneath the castle black smoke bubbled and boiled up. The smoke swirled and took on the form of a crone as old as time. Ereshkigal, the Black Witch had come up from the underworld. "Kill him now, my boy while his soul is alight with his love for his mate and at its strongest."

The Black Dragon aimed his own fire at his feet, burning his flesh until he could break his bones and free himself from the metal bonds. He sucked up the smoke around the Black Witch and spewed a black fire, not at Match, but at Fallyn.

Shit. This was going to hurt.

WITCHES AND BITCHES

The mermaid shouted at Match. "Fallyn and I are more than happy to take this asshole out on our own."

A wave of water carried Azynsa into the circle of fire Match had created to keep the humans of this area away from the battle. She shot fountains of water from her hands melting demon wyrms all around.

"Blue Witch." Fallyn acknowledged the mermaid carefully. "Have you come to kill me?"

"Not if I don't have to. We used to be friends. Sort of. We're here to rescue your ass."

Excellent. She wasn't here to kill Fallyn. She hadn't been sure. The last time she'd seen the Blue Witch, she'd been very angry. Mami Wata were strange beings, but with powerful control over the element of water. Especially if they were also a daughter of dragons.

Fallyn continued to use her skill of burning the wyrms from the inside out and making their heads explode. It wasn't quite as satisfying as sending her fire into that ice cream cone.

The Black Dragon roared and screeched and flapped his wings, trying to get free from the metal. More demon wyrms popped up out of the shadows of the trees and the castle wall. *Kill him and get his shard, my sons.*

My soul shard does you no good if I'm dead, Kur-Jara.

He was right. Unless Ereshkigal stole his soul.

Smoke bubbled and boiled up from a dark tunnel with the scent of Hell in it, under the castle. The smoke swirled and Fallyn's second worst nightmare appeared from the black magic. Ereshkigal, the Black Witch had come up from the underworld. "Kill him now, my boy while his soul is alight with his love for his mate and at its strongest."

The Black Dragon aimed his own fire at his feet, burning his flesh until he could break his bones and free himself from the metal bonds. He sucked up he smoke around the Black Witch and Fallyn's heart stopped beating. Kur-Jara had used this trick before. She remembered now. He laced his fire with the darkest cast offs from Ereshkigal's magic creating a devastating black fire.

The taint of that dark magic had almost killed Match when he'd put himself in the line of fire to save her from Kur-Jara's wrath.

She'd asked The Mother to save him with her light.

It was all happening again.

The painted Christmas ornament she'd carefully carried all afternoon crashed to the ground and shattered into a million pieces. Her own heart would fare no better if Match fell to the Black Dragon and she didn't save him.

Match dove from his place in the sky and threw himself between Kur-Jara and Fallyn. He would sacrifice himself for her. She had to be his savior, but she didn't know how.

Azynsa grabbed Fallyn and shot a stream of water filled with the light of love, blocking the black fire. Match flew straight through the liquid and came out the other side sputtering but alive.

Fallyn's heart practically burst out of her chest with that first beat returning to normal.

Match was safe, for now.

"You are going down, bitch." Azy pointed a finger at Ereshkigal. She'd said words similar aimed at her before. Fallyn wasn't sure if she and the Blue Witch were friends or enemies. There were a lot of people in her life she felt the same about.

Match for one. The Gold Dragon flying around throwing sunshine like he had an unending supply for another.

But if Azynsa wanted to hurt Ereshkigal, Fallyn was on board. "Bitch."

She liked this word. It had a harsh sound coming out of her mouth and that suited the woman who'd lied to her about everything for so long. There was a time when Fallyn had thought Ereshkigal was her mother. Kur-Jara had laughed at her when she'd asked him why her mother hated her so much.

Your mother was a fool who fell for a dragon, little redling. A stupid human who is long since dead. Let that be a lesson to you.

Ereshkigal didn't even acknowledge her or Azynsa. She was focused solely on Kur-Jara and Match. That was a mistake because Fallyn knew what to do to send the bitch back to Hell.

"Azynsa," she said the mermaid's name carefully so as to convey their alliance. "Tell your dragon to flood this whole area with his sunshine. Ereshkigal cannot abide the light and will retreat to where she came from."

Fallyn pointed toward the tunnel. "Kur-Jara will follow. He cannot claim the Red Warrior's soul shard without Ereshkigal to take the soul."

"She can fucking do that?" Water pooled around the woman's feet. "Take someone's soul?"

"Yes, she tried with your son." Fallyn didn't add that he was this close to being the sacrifice but without a savior. The mermaid was angry enough already.

Azynsa did not like that. She started marching toward Ereshkigal, water shooting like angry little fountains everywhere. "Ooh. I am going to cut her."

Fallyn grabbed her arm the same way Azynsa had to save her life. "That won't work. She is impervious to mortal weapons."

"Fine. But before the next time we see this god-damned fucking whore bag queen of the dead, you are going to tell me how to hurt her and hurt her bad." The mermaid was vibrating with her rage, a lot like Fallyn's necklace.

Hopefully Azynsa had learned to harness her anger and use it to fuel her power over the water because they were going to need a whole river's full for this plan to work. "Yes. I would like that. But we are not ready for the final battle yet. The Red Warrior still needs his mate. If we try to restore the balance between light and dark--"

"Yeah, yeah. Get on with your plan."

Fallyn took a step back so the mermaid's water did quench her own fire. "Flood the tunnel with the river. Push her back to hell with your elements."

"That's it? I can fucking do that. Why didn't you just say so?" Azynsa continued to grumble, saying something about grumpy bastards needing to learn how to romance a lady. She cupped her hands and shouted up to her Gold Dragon. "Hey, baby, light this motherfucker up like the fourth of July. Oh wait, that's only in America. Like Bastille Day. Damn, that's just France. Like Chinese New Year. Whatever, you get the point."

Rays of sun rained down to the ground and Fallyn's stomach turned. She'd been raised in darkness and the power of the light from the sun so bright was hard to handle. Just like the Queen of the Underworld. She had nowhere to retreat since her plan called for filling every nook and cranny with Ereshkigal's only weakness.

A dark blob floated toward her and she squinted trying to see if it was friend or foe. "Cover your eyes, *biedronka*, and hide your face from the harsh rays."

Match pulled her into his arms and pressed her head to his chest. She should have closed her eyes, but the sparkling red light from his soul shard was too pretty to pull her gaze away from. She heard the splashing of water and the curses of both the witch and the dragon as they retreated from the fight.

When she could hear them no more, the light faded and all that was left was the warm summer night, small fires burning away the remaining ashes of the demon wyrms, and the ruins of the metal dragon. "You can open your eyes now."

Fallyn looked up into the face of the warrior she'd known for so long was her enemy. The one she'd battled, the one she'd saved.

Mine.

Was that the voice she was supposed to listen to? "Did you hear that?"

"I don't hear anyone but you." Match's eyes flicked from hers down to her lips and back.

For some reason that made her stomach flip flop. Except the feeling wasn't in the same place as where she felt hunger or illness. It was lower.

"Fallyn. I'm going to kiss you. I'd like to kiss you a dozen times, but I'll start with one. If after that, you don't want me to kiss you some more, tell me to stop. I won't want to, but I will if you ask me to." The dragon's fire burned in his eyes and his soul shard's light matched it.

The necklace at her own throat vibrated, but there was no more danger for it to signal. This time it was communicating something else. It was angry and wanted her to do its bidding. She would figure out later what it wanted. Right now, she was busy.

Her breath caught in her throat and for a moment, as he lowered his mouth to hers, she forgot how to make her lungs work. Luckily for her Match breathed fire into their kiss. The flames licked along her lips and tongue, into her body and jump started her heart and soul.

He wrapped his arms around her back and waist, protecting her in the shelter of his arms. She didn't know what to do, but her body did. Her hands threaded into his hair, her leg wrapped around the back of one of his, and she leaned into his body.

His fire ignited her own and she tentatively released it to see if he liked the feel of it the way she did. He groaned so deep in his chest the sound must have come from his dragon. Red Dragons did love fire.

His grip on her waist tighten and he pressed his hips forward matching their centers together. Her insides were as hot as lava and she wanted her whole body to go up in his flames.

"Well, it's about fucking time. I'd tell you two to get a room, but I think the fire brigade is on their way here and it would probably be best if we weren't." The Gold Dragon's words filtered in through the flames but only partially made sense to her.

Match must have understood them though because he broke his lips from hers and touched their foreheads together instead. That was nice, but not as nice as the kissing. "Do you want more, or do I stop?"

She wanted much, much more. But she felt wrong for thinking that. He shouldn't be doing this with anyone but his mate.

Mine.

"I hate to break up a sure thing, gang. But we really have to leave. Like right now. Azy, my love. Why don't you take Fallyn with you for a little girl talk and Match and I will take care of the authorities. See you at home?" The Gold Dragon tapped Match on the shoulder.

Azynsa put one hand gently on Fallyn's arm. "Why do I always get stuck with the birds and bees while you get to yuck it up with your boys? Fine. But you two are talking to Apollo. I'm not explaining birth control to him."

"Yes, my love. But you do know dragons can't get sexually transmitted diseases and those flimsy things you call condoms cannot contain--"

Match shrugged the Gold Dragon off and pulled Fallyn away from the couple. "I don't want to leave your side, but the Gold is right. We have a mess to clean up here. Will you travel with Azynsa to their home? I promise to be there as soon as I can."

She wanted to ask if when they met again there would be

more kissing. She didn't, only nodded her head. Her thoughts and actions couldn't be trusted at the moment, so it was best to separate herself from him.

Leaving Kraków behind worried her. What if the voice in her head was Match's true mate and she was here? When she left, either he wouldn't find her, which would be bad, or he would. That was even worse.

She definitely did not understand these thoughts and feelings running around in her head like... like... the fallen. They had all acted and sounded like crazy beasts who couldn't make up their minds when they'd finally found their dragons. And they thought she was the one that was insane.

Maybe everyone who called her crazy were right. Azynsa had said there was something wrong with her more than once. If they were friends, Fallyn could ask her about how to not be that way and then she could quit acting all weird and get back to her mission.

With Ereshkigal's appearance on the Earth, the balance of dark and light was falling more and more out of alignment, out of balance. If the final battle didn't come soon, there would be no stopping her and her deep need for revenge would destroy them all.

Fallyn didn't know what to say to Match, so she simply walked away. But that didn't feel right, so she ran back to him touched her fingers to her lips and then to his.

"Oh my God, will you two just do it already and put the rest of us out of our misery?" The Gold Dragon threw his arms up and his head back like he was about to call down the light again. He must still have the battle lust in his blood.

Match stared down at her with some kind of emotion in his eyes that she didn't understand but wanted to. He answered Cage's strange question, but in the quietest of whispers so that only she could hear. "Not yet."

"Ugh. Come on, Fallyn. I'm guessing you don't want to travel by water. Good thing I got me a sugar dragon, because we are chartering a jet or a helicopter, or the space shuttle, and flying home in style. I cannot wait another minute to see my babies. I about slapped Match for making that calling all dragons rally cry. Do you even know how hard it is to get an appointment at Rime Arodaky in Paris for a custom Wolf Dress for a young bride to be? Isolda is going to kill me for coming home without one."

She followed Azynsa away from the dragons and to the nearby street. Azy held out her arm and a small Urus stopped for her. That was some fancy magic that Fallyn would like to learn.

Once they were both in and Azy told the man where to go, something called an air port, the woman turned to her and took one of her hands. "Okay, look, Fallyn. You and me, we've had our ups and downs. Isolda says you helped her and Apollo, so I'm not mad at you about the whole growing up overnight thing anymore. The White Witch on the other hand can bite me."

Fallyn didn't know how to reply to that. The Blue Witch's Dragon had already bitten her. It was good to know the two of them would not be at odds. "I don't think she would do that."

The Witch laughed. "Probably not. I just get mad, you know?"

"I know. I am mad too." But not as much as she was only a day ago.

"Yeah. I bet you are. I know your brain works, uh, different than the rest of us, and you don't always understand the ways of the human world or even the dragon world. I've been there done that when the Mami Wata came to get me when my dad died. I think we need to talk about some things. You up for that?"

This seemed like they were going to friends for now. "What do you want to talk about, Blue Witch?"

"Let's start with that. You know my name, girlfriend. Call me Azy. People weird out when they hear the word witch." Her eyes flicked to the driver, but he was only paying attention to the other Urus's on the road.

Match had also wanted her to say his name. Why were their names and not what they did so important? Their powers over the elements were much more important. But the Blue Witch, Azynsa, was asking something that was not hard to give. "Okay. I will try to remember that."

"Good. Here's another thing, and this one is kind of important, so pay attention." Azynsa narrowed her eyes. "You can't go around stabbing people."

Azynsa must be confused. "I can't let the demon wyrms--"

Azy held up a hand to stop her words. "Those little rat bastards aren't people. They are fair game. You murder as many of them as you like and have fun doing it. But no trying to kill humans, witches, wolves, or dragons."

That was going to make killing the Black Dragon and ending Ereshkigal's reign of terror hard. "I can't make that promise to you. I have vowed to bring balance between good and evil. When the final battle comes--"

Azy stopped her again. "Nope. I see where you're going, and I don't mean the fucking Black Dragon. He needs to die a horrible death, so does that bitch witch. I'm talking about my family and friends, sugar. You can't try to kill Cage or Match, or any of their mates."

"Oh." She understood the request now. She'd done a lot of stabbing to keep herself safe from the Dragons, from Match. "I don't want to kill them."

"I saw." Azy winked at her. "You sleeping with that sexy beast? You be doing the world a favor because, whoo boy, does that grumpy ass man need to get laid, but hearts will be breaking all over the world if you take him off the market."

"I don't understand most of what you said." This woman was right, Fallyn didn't understand the human or dragon world very well. But she did know she had to save it.

"Damn. I thought not." Azy glanced up at the driver who didn't seem to be paying them any attention, then she lowered her voice. "Fallyn, are you a virgin?"

LOVE'S LONG GAME

Cage was one slick son of a dragon. He was infinitely better at dealing with the humans than Match ever was. In minutes he had the authorities convinced that the two of them had witnessed an explosion of the gas line that gave the Wawel Dragon the ability to shoot fire and that the city officials were lucky no one had been hurt, thanks to him and Match.

Match would have just given the whole lot of humans wads of cash. That usually shut them up.

That had taken much less time than he'd imagined and now he was irritated he'd sent Fallyn off with Azynsa. The two of them had a tumultuous relationship and he couldn't be sure they wouldn't kill or maim each other. That wasn't the real reason he was off kilter.

The moment Fallyn had walked away from him, his heart ached for her. Not in the way it had for the last hundred years. This emptiness in his chest was new. It didn't hurt like it had before. Now it was more like hunger, and hunger could be satisfied in a way his loneliness never could.

"Let's fly, Cage. We can hide in the darkness of the riverbed. I want to catch up to the women as soon as possible." Match brought his dragon to the surface and prepared to shift.

Cage simply stood there, crossed his arms and stared him down. "Yeah. I'm sure you do. I'm not going to be the dick and ask if you know what you're doing with Fallyn. Your soul shard is burning so bright I need sunscreen. But I think there's something you need to know before you go all crazy claiming her and bringing her into our battle with the Black Dragon and the Queen of the Underworld."

"She is my mate. I know everything I need to know." It wasn't like he was going to ask Cage for sex advice. He was the Wyvern who'd once lost his soul shard to a succubus because he'd been a horny bastard.

Not that Match wasn't horny. His dick was ready to bust out of his leathers every time he even smelled Fallyn, or looked at Fallyn, or thought of Fallyn. He couldn't wait to give her a dozen orgasms at least. Then a dozen more. His years of celibacy were worth the wait. For her.

But Cage had taken on the mantle of AllWyvern, a position that was traditionally held by a Red Dragon Warrior. Match had ceded to Cage since his children and mate had been in danger and Match had needed to focus on tracking Fallyn down. The Gold had done well in leading the united Dragon Wyrs against the forces of evil. He took the position very seriously and was probably worried that his most powerful ally was about to mate with someone he'd thought of as an enemy.

"Don't worry, brother. I'm sure Fallyn will find the White Witch's ring and you can officiate in our mating ceremony."

He could hardly wait to see her Wyvern's mate ring on her finger.

"I know you think this is a sure thing, man. But a group of my warriors that were trapped in hell have come out mated to succubae. Fucking bane of my existence. They've come to me with intel from their time spent under Geshtianna's thumb." Cage spit the former succubus Queen's name like the foul thing it was.

"There is nothing you or any succubus could tell me that would change my mind about Fallyn." He'd known his secrets would have to come to light eventually. It was either now or in the final battle that all would be revealed. Match didn't care either way, but it was clear Cage was going to be a dick about it.

"I hate to admit it, but Portia's succubae are damn good spies and they brought us a major tip that we could use to turn the tide back in our favor." Cage paused and stared back at the burning rubble of the battle and the tunnel to Hell. "The Black Dragon is after your soul shard. Fallyn is leading him right to you."

"Of course he is. He's attempted to steal everyone else's, why not mine? I am the only Wyvern left who has not given my soul to my mate yet." Something he intended to fix immediately if not sooner.

"Because he thinks yours is the only one that can restore his soul." Cage thought he had the killing blow with that information. Gold's loved to think they knew everything. Usually they did. Just not about this.

Match shouldn't be surprised Cage's spy network had found that vital bit of information. It was good intel. "Ah. Well. He is right."

"You mother-fucker." Scales flittered across Cage's face and his eyes shifted to that of his dragon. "You'd better start talking or I'm going to go all sunshine on your ass. I am not losing my kids because you're keeping shit from me."

Match's dragon bristled at the threat, but it was fair. Cage had a hell of a lot to lose. He was the only living Dragon warrior with children and the battle for their little souls had begun even before their birth. Match wasn't a completely selfish prick. He would do what he must to ensure the future of all Dragonkind.

The part of him that had been bathed in the importance of the Red Dragon Wyr's secrets balked at the telling. But it was time. "It is the duty of all Red Dragons to keep the rest of our brethren safe from the darkness of our forefather's failures. You may be the AllWyvern, but I am the sacrifice that will end this war, and Fallyn is the savior of us all."

"Fuck me." Cage turned his back on him and walked away. He flailed his arms about shouting curses in all kinds of languages, several he must have learned from his mate who was quite efficient at swearing. It took a few minutes, but he finally calmed back down and returned to the conversation as cool as a cucumber and cream cheese sandwich. He pointed a finger at Match. "I officially call an AllWyr council. You can present your mate to the other Wyverns and explain every single god-damned thing you know about ending this war."

"Fine. But only after I have claimed my mate."

By the time Match and Cage got to the airport, Azy and Fallyn were already in the air in a private jet almost as big as a dragon. Certainly not as fast. Cage insisted on calling in a fleet of his Golds to escort the plane while the two of them flew ahead to the Gold Wyr's headquarters on the Spanish coast.

They would have their AllWyr council and by the time the mates landed he would be free of his responsibilities to his brother Wyverns. Normally it took days to convene the other Wyverns since Ky Puru had to swim over from the Antipodes, but all three of the other Wyverns were already in Spain along with their mates and their seconds. Even half the Troika pack had come over from America.

Seemed like everyone except for him had been invited to the wedding of Cage's daughter Isolda to the heir of the alpha of the Troika wolf pack. They were babies only yesterday, or last month. Today, they were full grown, be it young, adults and were ready to mate for life. Match was probably the only among the guests that understood how young love felt. He wished these two better luck than he and Fallyn had been given.

Given their speedy ascent into adulthood at the hand of Fallyn and her declarations that they were needed for the coming final battle, he doubted fate would be kind to them either. He would do his best to help them through the troubled times ahead even if Cage hadn't seen fit to invite him to their wedding.

It's not like the human ceremony was the same as the Dragon Warrior's mating ritual.

The mates were all gathered in Isolda's bedroom. Even if he hadn't been told, Match would be able to tell by the squeals and laughter coming from that side of the estate. The other Wyverns and the wolf alphas were in the kitchen. Drinking.

"'Sup, boss." Geez. Even Dax had been invited to the nuptials. He handed Match a bottle of beer. "I brought these schmoes some Zywiec so they could get a taste of the real deal instead of their local swill."

"I'll take a good Czech Pilsner Urquell over your trashy little brewery anytime, Red." Jacob, the Green Wyvern, and his second, Steele raised their bottles and clinked.

Cage rooted around in the freezer and brought out a bottle of hard liquor. "I'm gonna need something a whole lot stronger than beer after talking to this asshole all night. You Troika boys don't mind if I break out your vodka, do you?"

When Cage laid out the shot glasses, the wolf alphas each took one. Niko, the Wolf Tzar held his aloft. "To you fucking dragons, welcome to the family, assholes. *Za zdaróvye.*"

Cage threw his shot back, poured another and slammed his glass down on the counter to get everyone's attention. "Let's get down to business. Wolves, normally I'd ask you to get out, but since Max's son is about to become my son-in-law, you can stay."

"Like you could kick us out." Max poured everyone another round.

"Right. I declare this AllWyr and uh, AllPack. We've got some messy business to discuss and everyone's favorite asshole here has been keeping shit from us that could potentially end our war with Hell."

Dax set his beer bottle down and stepped between Match and the rest of the alphas in the room. He was a good kid, barely into his Prime and newly mated. He would make a good Wyvern someday soon. Steel, Zon and Gris, Taika, and Neo, the other seconds all stood to protect their Wyverns as well.

"I respectfully request you keep your accusations to yourself, AllWyvern. The Red Wyr has killed more Demon Wyrms and protected the people of the world safe from their evil plague a hell of a lot longer and better than the rest of you." Ever loyal to the Wyr. Yes, Match had chosen his new Second Wyvern well.

The room exploded into grumbles and more accusations. This solved nothing. Match took another sip of his beer and waited for his brothers to get over themselves. Eventually all eyes turned on him since he wasn't in the fray of it all.

"You Reds are secretive assholes. You should have told us about Fallyn. How long have you known she's your mate?" Cage air quoted the word known.

Match's dragon did not like anyone questioning him or his mate. He'd be happy to take the Gold down a notch, make him remember who the alpha of alphas truly was. That would take up time he didn't want to waste. When Fallyn arrived, the rest of the Wyverns and alphas could do whatever the fuck they wanted. He was claiming his mate.

"The Red Dragons have always kept the secrets of Dragonkind, and we trust few." The room went quiet at his words. Cage and the other Wyverns were good Dragon Warriors, their hearts and souls were true. They were his brothers in all things. These wolves were doing their best to change their part of the world for the better and while he'd never admit it out loud, he liked them.

He'd never revealed this part of his failure to anyone save his own father and hoped he never had to. An alpha led by example. Match had often felt like a shitty leader. Match had to make sure Dax was a better one and the way to do that was to lead by example.

It was not in his DNA to ask for help, forgiveness, or grace for his mistakes. But he was about to.

He didn't care what anyone else thought of him. He knew the truth of who and what he was. If it meant the difference between the other Wyverns trusting his mate so they could all work together and defeat the Black Dragon, he would confess the dark mark on his soul. He would not give up Fallyn. Not when they had such a short time to be together. The sooner he got this explanation over with, the sooner he could be with her again.

"I marked Fallyn over a hundred and fifty years ago." A wound in his heart that had been open and bleeding his whole life ached with the memory.

"You have got to be shitting me," Ky said.

Jakob nodded. "You were what, like in your forties, barely out of diapers?"

Zon asked, "Had you even gotten your soul shard yet, learned to shift?"

Gris shook his head. "A dragonling would not know his mate. No way."

The only one who stayed silent was Jett. The Black Demon Dragon Wyvern was new among the AllWyr. He was older than them all, the bastard son of the First Dragon and an Annunaki demon. He'd spent his entire life in Hell. He'd been raised side by side with Fallyn. Of them all, he likely knew the most bits of this story.

"I knew the first day I saw her, when we were both only children, that she was mine and I was hers. It wasn't until I got my shard that I knew what to do about it." It hadn't mattered that his father had explained the Dragon Warriors of his generation were cursed and could no longer find their mates.

"The witch came to our house and pulled that shard of my soul. I remember thinking it was strange because all my friends had their shards pulled by a local red witch who barely had any power at all. But I believe the woman who came to our house that day was the White Witch. I marked Fallyn that very day."

Ky made a face. "This isn't gonna get creepy, is it, bro?"

"Don't be an ass. I didn't know my dick from my arm at that age. I merely bit her, giving her my mark, and promised to build her castle." And promised her his soul. "Then we went to my birthday party. She baked me a szarlotka."

Kosta took the bottle from Max and poured more shots. "I'm completely uncomfortable with how mushy gushy you look right now."

Cage was still angry, the tone of his voice made that very apparent. "So why the fuck have we all been chasing our tails over mates if you broke the curse before the rest of us were even talking?"

The scar over the gaping hole in his heart itched and ached. "Fallyn died. Killed in a battle with the demon wyrms."

"I knew this was going to get creepy. She's a fucking zombie," Ky declared.

Jakob looked over at Jett for confirmation. "A ghost? Some kind of demon?"

"Fallyn was and is as human as Ciara," was all he said.

Match nodded. "Her mother was from a long line of Romani red witches and that's where she got her power over fire. Her aunts were the ones who'd pulled my friend's shards."

"So, what? She's been reincarnated as the Black Dragon's daughter?" Ky was the first of them to encounter Fallyn in Hell when he went to recover Cage's soul shard. That seemed like a long time ago now. He clapped Match on the arm. "That's some fucked up shit, bro. What the hell did you Reds do to deserve that?"

Jett interjected. "He is not her father any more than he is mine."

Match swallowed down the memory that threatened to bring him to his knees. "I did not know who or what he was at the time, but Kur-Jara kidnapped Fallyn that day and took her to Hell."

"Fuck."

Match didn't know which Dragon Warrior had said that, but he understood the sentiment to his core.

"I failed to protect her then, and I failed her for the next hundred and fifty years. I should have known she was still alive and spent my entire life trying to rescue her."

"If you had all of you would probably all be dead now." Fallyn walked into the kitchen alongside Azy. "Kur-Jara would have stolen your soul and used it to make Hell on Earth. I will never let that happen. Even if it means I have to fall for you."

FALLING FOR FALLYN

*K*illing Dragons was bad. Stabbing was bad. But so was the way the room full of alpha warriors were all looking at her. Were they all staring at her like they had daggers in their eyes because she'd just admitted her weakness in falling for Match?

The other Dragon's mates were not weak. But they had fallen.

That must not be why everyone looked like they wanted to destroy her. Everyone except Match. He was...smiling. She'd never seen him do that before. Like, she could see his shiny white teeth and everything.

"She's not going to ruin our kid's wedding, is she?" one of the wolf alphas asked.

Hmm. He was the father of Ellie and Tristan. The wolves saw darkness better than most other creatures in the world. She'd discovered that when she'd helped the wolf twins grow into their adult bodies. Their training had been easier than Apollo's and Izzy's. They recognized not only the dark in

Ereshkigal's minions, but in Fallyn herself, and they were scared of neither.

They would fulfill their duties well as saviors and sacrifices.

No, the wolves did not have as much mad on for her as the Dragons. She re-examined what she said that might have set them on edge.

Ah. She got it. If she fell for Match, then they must believe she is not his true mate. They wanted this mystery woman who would not reveal herself to fall for Match so they can all battle to restore the balance between light and dark.

This woman was not here. She would not show herself. Fallyn would have to step up and take her place. That was not her intention, and she prayed that she could fulfill the role the Red Witch was supposed to have, but she didn't see any other choice. Now that Ereshkigal and Kur-Jara knew how to find the Red Warrior and his soul shard, they would not stop until they had it or Kur-Jara died trying.

Fallyn fingered the daggers strapped to her thighs. They were not as easy to access in the new clothes Azynsa had acquired for her and made her change into before their plane took off for the Gold Dragon's villa. But they were softer than anything else she'd ever worn before. Silk, it was called. Not good for battle, but more comfortable for the ride in the flying machine.

Azynsa had said she shouldn't stab any of her friends, but she would defend herself.

"*Biedronka*." Match set down a bottle and walked toward her in long room consuming strides. Every other alpha in the room moved to the side to clear a path for him. His soul shard shined bright filling the room with brilliant fiery light. The necklace at her throat shimmied against her skin like it was trying to jump up and reach for him.

He grabbed her up in his arms, dipped her back, and kissed her right there in front of all the other dragons and alphas. He kissed her and kissed her and kissed her just like he said he would. She didn't even think about asking him to stop.

Every cell in her body lit up with a tingling, sparkling fire. She wanted this. Screw that bitch who wouldn't come to be by his side. She didn't know what she was missing.

A sudden calm spread through her, not dousing her fires, but banking them slighty, and new voices joined the grumbling groans of the men in the room. "Hey, why don't you ever kiss me like that, Jakey-poo."

"I hope Tristan kisses me like that at our wedding." The lilting voice of a young woman pushed its way into Fallyn's mind. Like it had a hundred thousand times before.

"I do not. I'd prefer a chaste kiss on the cheek, and nothing more on your wedding day." That was Azynsa.

Fallyn wished they all go away.

"Silly mermaid," Izzy said and laughed.

Fallyn placed one hand on Match's cheek and gently pulled her lips and tongue from the dance with his. She didn't want to stop kissing Match, but Izzy, who was the only friend she'd had for her long years in Hell, even if she had only been in her head, was here in the flesh. She'd only briefly gotten to see her in the battle for the wolf pup's souls. She'd like to say thank you to the one person who'd helped her find her way in the darkness of Hell. There was a time that Izzy felt more like her sister.

"I'm not ready to let you go, love." Match whispered the words only for her to hear. "Let me take you away from all these people and show you exactly what it means to be fated mates."

Oh. She didn't know exactly what he meant, but the way he said it made her feel achy and needy somewhere deep inside. Maybe she could talk to Izzy later.

"Oh no you don't, you grumpy bastard. The mates have voted, and by mates, I mean me." The words seemed angry, but the voice was light and happy. Only one mate Fallyn knew of could do such funny things with emotions like that. "Azy says Fallyn has some, uh, missing parts of her education and you aren't taking her anywhere until we can fill some of them in."

A little wrinkle formed between Match's eyebrows and he stood, still holding her tight in his arms. "Ciara, just because I like you doesn't mean you can keep my mate from me. Don't you have a wedding to plan?"

The Green Wyvern's mate who embodied the powers of a white witch wrinkled up her nose and shook her finger at them. "Good try, buddy. But it's all arranged. What I have to plan now is a Wyvern's mating ceremony. Don't I?"

Match's chest and arms tensed. "Shit. Jakob--"

"Nope. Don't even think about telling me to control my mate. You should know better by now." The Green Wyvern took the hand of his mate and kissed it.

It had been a long time since Fallyn had heard this particular witch's voice in her head. She'd been the first to fall, well before Fallyn had needed to help. She was special this one. A direct descendant of the Mother. Just like Ellie and Tristan's mother.

"Hiya, Fallyn. I don't know if you remember me." The white witch held out her hand.

"Hello, White Witch." She took the witch's hand and immediately felt the surge of her power. Her own fire responded, dancing along her skin and jumping over to Match and back.

"That's a new one on me. I thought the Goddess was the White Witch. I mean, I guess I am one, but you can call me Ciara. I'd like to be friends if we can." Nothing in the world could be sad or bad or wrong when she spoke. Such an interesting feeling.

The White Witch's powers were bringing up emotions Fallyn didn't know she had. Things she didn't know she wanted. She was finding it hard to keep her guard up around these people. "Ciara. I don't have any friends so I don't know how to be that."

"Uh, what am I, chopped tuna?" Azynsa waved her hand.

"You are the mother of a sacrifice and a savior. You are the Blue Witch. You are the fallen mate of the Gold Dragon. I thought you knew that. I will go back to calling you by your powers so you don't forget again. It's important that you know what to do in the final battle."

"And what are you, Fallyn?" Ciara asked.

No one had ever asked her that. Not Ereshkigal, not Kur-Jara, not Jett, not even Match. "I'm....nothing important."

Match whipped her around. "You're Fallyn Ejderhaninkizi, the mate of the Red Dragon Wyvern, you're the Red Witch, you're the love of my life."

Fallyn's hands shook and her heart felt like it was going to come out of her chest. She wanted to be all of those things. So badly it hurt. Or maybe it didn't. Whatever was happening deep in her soul wasn't painful. Different, but not painful.

His mate. His love.

"Hey, you two have got that schmexy times are coming

look. I'm serious, Match. You want to let us give Fallyn the, uh, talk, before you, you know." Ciara was already talking quite a bit, so Fallyn didn't know what else they needed to say to her.

"I can handle this just fine without your help, Ciara." Match addressed the witch, but didn't take his eyes off of hers.

She was getting lost in those eyes.

Another woman with a powerful aura giggled and snorted. "Ciara. I think she'll be fine. It's not like I'd done the deed before Jett and I--"

The rest of her words were muffled. "Yvaine. No one here needs to hear about our sex-life."

"You're a party pooper. But I already knew that and I love you anyway. How about you and I go to our room and they can hear about it anyway."

A lot of the other people in the room groaned. Azynsa clapped her hands three times and quieted them all down. "Enough. All of you, my lovely daughter is in the room. It's late and I suggest we all retire and reconvene by the light of day."

"I'll make cinnamon rolls and bacon for breakfast," the Summer Shadow said.

"Fallyn you schedule in girl talk with us in the morning and I don't want to hear any argument." Azynsa pointed at the two of them. "Match, our biggest fireplace is in the west wing, last door at the end of the hall. It's bright red, so you can't miss it. You be good to that girl or Imma have to cut you and poison your coffee. You hear me?"

"I swear it on my life." Match lifted her hand and kissed it. Which wasn't as lovely as his kisses to her mouth, but nice just the same.

"Okay. Good. Then everybody get the hell out of my kitchen. Cage, take me to bed or lose me forever."

Cage picked up Azynsa and threw her over his shoulder so her butt was sticking straight up in the air. He smacked it and walked toward the exit. "Great balls of fire."

"Oh my God. My parents are so weird. I'm going to play video games with Tristan and Apollo. Good night, Fallyn. I hope we get a chance to hang out tomorrow." Izzy left but in the opposite direction of Azynsa and Cage.

Almost everyone else left, a few with pats to Match's back or light slugs to his arms. Ciara didn't move and smiled strangely at the two of them.

"Ciara, *milacek*. Quit being a perv or I'm going to have to blindfold you." Jakob dragged Ciara out of the kitchen too.

"Oh, goody," she said and winked at Fallyn as they too left.

The power in the room faded and Fallyn took a long, deep breath. "I'm glad they're all gone. I've never been in such a small space with so many Dragon Warriors, wolves, demons, and witches before."

"Don't forget the unicorn."

"She is unforgettable. Even for me. What do they mean by girl talk? They all talk out loud so much. I like the quiet with you." A flash of a memory when he'd been her peace before, somewhere far away, with apple trees and dappled light and promises of castles and love. It couldn't be her memory, but she wanted it to be.

He took a long slow breath that matched hers. "*Beidronka,* come, sit down at the counter here. Let me make you something to eat."

She was hungry. She was always hungry. This ache in her

stomach felt different than the need for food. "I can wait for the Summer Shadow's baked goods to break my fast."

"Please, Fallyn. Sit." He motioned toward some soft padded stools on the other side of a stone counter. "I want to feed you. It hurts my heart to think of how you must have gone without at the hands of Ereshkigal and Kur-Jara."

It hurt his heart? That sounded bad. Fallyn touched her palm to his chest, hoping it would soothe the pain. He swallowed hard and she saw in his gaze the truth of his words. He did hurt, but for her pain and suffering. "I will eat."

She sat and watched as her Red Warrior grabbed food from the cold box and set it out on a wooden board on the counter between them. He shifted several of his claws and sliced the foods into delicate pieces. "What is that one called?"

It was a greenish yellow on the outside and white on the inside. It smelled familiar, but she didn't think she'd ever eaten before.

"This fruit is a pear. Taste it." He picked up a slice and held it up to her lips, centimeters away from her mouth.

She could have taken it from him and fed herself, but there was something she liked about eating the food from his fingers. Fallyn carefully bit down and juice from the fruit surged into her mouth and over her lips. She chewed and darted her tongue out to catch the juicy dribbles. "That's delicious."

Match made a funny sound and licked his own lips, but he hadn't taken a bite of the pear. He held another slice of something yellowy-orange to her mouth this time. "Try this one."

She tried to take a bite, but Match slid the chunk across her lips, painting them with the juice. She had to dart her tongue out to get it from him and tasted not only the sweet and tart of the fruit, but the saltiness of the skin on his fingers.

She wasn't sure which tasted better. "I like that too. What's it called?"

"Huh?" Match was staring at her mouth. "Oh. That's a peach."

Her hunger was awakening like a tired beast that had been sleeping for a long time. "Do you have more for me?"

"So much more. But for now, we'll eat." Match chopped up the rest of the fruit and some cheese and a little meat. He set the wooden board next to her and then joined her on the seat next seat over.

Fallyn picked up a piece of cheese, she meant to put it in her own mouth, but she lifted her hand to his instead. Match parted his lips ever so slowly and let her place the bit of food between his teeth. He captured her hand before she could pull it away and closed his lips over her fingers.

The kiss to her fingers was almost as good as the ones to her lips. This made that hunger in her lower belly come to life and growl for more.

"Delicious." The word was a deep, low tone that sounded like it came from the depths of his soul. He kissed the tips again and then gently dropped her hand.

"The cheese or me?" Her own voice came out so breathy, like her voice was lost in a haze somewhere.

"Definitely you." Match picked up a slice of apple, that one she knew. He finished chewing and swallowed the cheese, then put the piece of apple half in his mouth, half hanging out. He leaned forward and touched the bit of apple to her lips.

A game. She never knew eating could be... fun. She bit at

the fruit, but he moved so her teeth snapped down on nothing.

She laughed. Oh. She'd never done that before either. She'd seen colorful little insects like nature's sparkling ornaments, when she'd stayed with Ninsy. She'd called them butter something. Butterflies. It was like butterflies flying around in her chest and coming out of her mouth. She was having a lot of firsts with Match.

He grinned at her and held the apple slice up between them neither closer to her mouth than his. "I know apples aren't new to you, don't you want a bite?"

"I do." Her wants were all jumbled up inside.

"Then don't wait any longer. You can have whatever you want from me, Fallyn."

She didn't know what she wanted, but she hoped he had whatever it was. Such a silly thing to think. She could be silly with him.

Fallyn licked her lips again and tipped her head forward. She just touched the apple and he snatched it away, replacing the flesh of the fruit with his own lips. The kiss was soft and teasing, not desperate like the last. He brushed his mouth across hers and dipped his tongue in and out, in a way that had her whimpering with need.

For what she didn't know. For more of him she supposed.

All of him, for all of her.

He smiled against her lips. "The apple could not have tasted sweeter than your kiss, my love."

Love. There had been such talk of this. How could she understand it if she'd never experienced it. "Do you love me?"

"I always have. I always will. Even when we are separated

for a hundred years or more. I have loved you for all those year and I will love you and only you for all time."

Her heart beat so fast. "I want to say the same, but I do not know what it means to love."

How can she love when she was afraid to fall?

How could she be as brave as all the other mates?

LOVE'S FIRES

*H*is Fallyn was so fierce, so brave. She was going against everything she'd ever learned, ever experienced to follow her instincts even though she was sure it would lead to pain and her own destruction.

He didn't deserve her, but he would spend every minute they had together proving to her that love was what they both needed.

"Let me show you. Love is more than what the body can do, more than what I can give you this night. When you give yourself to me and let me mark you, claim you, and make you my mate, we join our souls and make each other stronger."

She nodded gravely like pieces of a puzzle were putting themselves together and she didn't exactly like the picture. "Is that love? Giving up your soul to another to make them strong?"

Her questions punched him straight in the gut. "No, *biedronka*, you don't have to give up anything. Love doesn't take, it gives you more. It's sharing your heart and your soul.

Two become one, but the one is more than the two ever were apart."

How could he explain love? That's what he'd been taught. His mother might not have been his father's fated mate, but he had loved her and never taken another companion after she died. He'd seen the same deep emotions in each of his brother Wyverns as they each found their mates.

He'd never actually experienced any of this for himself. He knew he loved Fallyn, without a doubt. But had he ever fallen in love himself? No. He just was already in love.

He hadn't understood any of his feelings back when they were young. The day he met her it was like the fire in his soul warmed everything else in his body, like he was hungry and couldn't be satisfied with any amount of food, like he was thirsty, and nothing could quench him. Like if he held her long enough nothing bad could ever happen in the world ever again. Only happiness.

But bad things had happened. The worst.

The fire never went away, nor the hunger. But the warmth and joy had. Nothing and no one ever brought the feeling back. Tonight, they could find it again together. "I'm not sure I know what falling in love means either. Let's find out together."

Fallyn put her hands on his cheeks, rubbing her fingers through the whiskers of his beard, and got the most beautiful wrinkle between her eyes that showed him how deeply she was thinking about his words. Her gaze flicked back and forth between his eyes, between his heart and his soul. "I feel like I'm falling. Is this what the other mates felt? Is this what it means to be fallen?"

He had no idea how anyone else felt because he'd been

angry for so long, he'd forgotten what anything else was. "Like your heart is bigger than your chest and it could fly if you let it?"

Her eyes lit up and went wide. "Yes, and like the whole world would fit inside, but never be filled."

Maybe both of them did know what falling in love felt like.

"Yes. Exactly like that. If this is what fallen means to you, then I've fallen for you." He was still falling, and he was going to crash hard.

"I thought only the mates fell, not the dragons. That it meant I would lose myself, but I've never been more... me than when I'm with you." Fallyn kissed him then, soft and tentative at first, then like she couldn't get enough of him.

He knew the feeling.

Match picked his mate up and took her to the room Cage and Azy had designed especially for visiting Red Dragons. He kicked the door open and carried her across the threshold, into their new future together.

He set her down next to the bed and ran a hand down through her hair to her throat and neck. "I'm going to make love to you, Fallyn. Join our bodies and our souls. I want you to know you're the only woman I've ever done this with. There has never been anyone else for me and there never will."

It was unlikely she understood how important that was to him. He'd purposefully learned the art of making a woman feel pleasure but had never fucked any of his willing teachers. His dragon and his dick knew she was the only woman he would ever share himself with.

He could only hope that he was the only man she'd ever be with too. He couldn't think about the harshness of what may have happened to her in hell if that wasn't true. There would be no talk of it now, because tonight was only about pleasure and love, but someday he would ask and eviscerate anyone who'd ever even dared to look at his Fallyn.

"I don't know what that means. But I've seen the other mates with their Warriors and if making love means touching and kissing and letting our souls dance in the light of the fire. I've never done that either, but I want to with you."

Thank the fates.

She turned her back to him and slowly slid the black silk tunic from her shoulders. Her long raven hair covered her skin, trailing all the way down to her round ass.

The bits of her skin he could see around her tresses was soft and dotted with freckles. He'd lick each and every one of them and couldn't wait to see if she had them between her legs too so he could lick them as well.

She shyly glanced over her shoulder at him, her hair swaying to the side. She was seductive and sensual without even knowing what those things were.

That's when he saw them. A thousand lash marks criss-crossing her back, one scar on top of another, on top of another.

Match very carefully skimmed his fingers over the marks, letting the roughness of her skin sink into his soul. Scales rippled across his hand, his Dragon wanting to burst forth and protect her from the pain these must have come from. He didn't want to think she was ugly for having them or that he'd love her body any less, so he tempered his tone to hide the anger inside. "Fallyn. What are these, what happened?"

He traced every one of the mars to her skin, wanting from the depths of his soul to take them from her, heal her. But he was no green dragon, and most of the wounds had been inflicted centuries before if he had to guess.

She bit her lip and looked away. "They are from my fa— Kur-Jara."

"He punished you with lashes?" Match had seen the Black Dragon's fire whip in battle. It physically hurt every fiber of his being that he'd used that weapon on Fallyn.

"No." She held her chin up. Her will would never be beaten. "They were his gift."

"A gift?" What had the sick bastard Black Dragon taught her?

"Yes. Pain is a gift, he said. One that showed me I was still alive. On my birthday he gave them to me. One for every year. He said I was lucky because the dragon's soul I'd touched made me age slower so I would have more birthdays, at least until I helped him find that soul and he could take it away."

The last time he'd seen her, a century and a half ago, she'd only been a child, about equivalent to a human five-year-old. He'd shared his soul with her when he marked her. It was because of him she aged like a dragon, as all true mates did when they were marked.

A hundred and fifty-five. That's how many lashes she'd have gotten this year. He couldn't even stomach that a small child would be lashed five or six times, but the fact that as a young woman she was struck with the slicing pain of the whip hundreds of times sucked the breath from his lungs.

She'd lived through a century of pain because of him. 'You don't have to be in pain like this ever again."

Fallyn shrugged one shoulder. "I don't know how to feel without it. That's all I've ever known."

He would do everything in his power to change that. But,

if pain was what she understood, the first step was trans-forming that pain into pleasure. That he could do.

"Let me show you a different kind of pain. One that still has the bite you need, but that will give you pleasure." His bite was exactly what he'd give her. She already wore his mark. But the tattoo on her skin was crude and immature, just as he'd been back then.

Match let her tunic fall to the floor and gave the loose-fitting pants a tug too. She stepped out of the clothes and didn't try to hide herself from him. His dragon ached to touch her, run his tongue along every crease and curve of her chest, hips, and thighs. If he didn't get to taste the exact place on her neck where she bore his mark soon, he was going to forget his own name.

He kissed his way up the back of her arm, tracing the scars there with his lips. Her breaths came in faster little gasps, the nearer he got to her neck. The red sparkling dragon tattoo wriggled and writhed as if excited for his return. Match scraped his teeth across her skin, and she groaned and shoved her hands into his hair.

"Do that again."

Like he could deny her anything. He teased her by rubbing the rough whiskers across her skin first and then soothed the burn with his tongue. Later, he would share his fire with her too. For now, just his bite.

Match found just the right spot, between her collar bone and her throat and sucked on the soft skin there. The dragon danced in his mouth begging him for more. His own Dragon responded with its own lusty need to mark his mate so no one would ever question who she belonged to ever again.

His dragon's fangs elongated in his mouth and he sank his

teeth into her skin. Fire poured out from his soul and into the oldest of scars on her body.

"Match, oh fires, don't stop. Give me more." Her body melted into his, her muscles relaxing, her knees giving out, and her arms wrapped around his neck to keep from falling.

He grabbed her under her legs and lifted her into his arms, never moving his mouth from where it was buried in her neck. She stilled in his arms and laid her head back giving him even more access to her throat. She was willingly making herself vulnerable to him.

The more fire he poured into her, the more powerful he felt. His soul shard burned against his skin screaming at him to claim her, mate her, and give her his soul.

Not yet. First, she needed to know that she was loved and that he was there to protect her and give her pleasure.

Match laid her on the bed and released his bite. He licked over the wound to soothe it, but the dragon would heal her soon enough. Any pain he'd caused her was laced with love and pleasure too. The flush of her skin, the rapid beat of her heart, and the scent of her arousal in the air told him he'd done what she needed.

He crawled over her and pressed a kiss to each of her eyes, hazy and lust filled for him. She blinked after each and touched the growing mark on her skin. With each passing second the dragon tattoo shifted and transformed from a crude red dragon to a complex and intricate Wyvern that mirrored his own dragon form.

The beast inside took pleasure in seeing its true form on her. But it wanted more. so much more.

"You must take your clothes off too, my Warrior. Let me

see your body and touch your scars too." She reached for his shirt and made quick work of the fastenings.

Her touch was intoxicating like the best alcohol laced with Dragon's Fire. Even as her fingers touched his old wounds, he wanted more. He had plenty of scars of his own, but his were trophies of battles with evil. Hers were too, but her battles hadn't been fought with claws and teeth, but her strong will alone. No one could have been stronger.

"Forget the past, Match." She touched the one small mark on his own skin that he'd never give up. The tiniest semi-circles where she'd bit him so many years ago. Lightning shot through his veins and he sucked in a slow breath to keep himself under control. She wanted to explore him, and he would not be an asshole by giving into his own lust.

She traced the outline and kissed the scar. "I can see how distracted you are by those thoughts. Don't go there. Be here with me, now."

"Not all of your past is filled with pain and evil." He swallowed down the bitter edge of anger. He rarely let himself think of his childhood before the attack. "Remind me someday to tell you about the castle we planned to build with the apple orchard in the back garden, of the days we spent playing in the forests, chasing fairies through the night, and sitting in the shade of nanny's big skirts drinking lemonade and eating szarlotka until our bellies were big like boulders full of the sweet life. Of the day I let you bite me to see if it would hurt."

It hadn't. Her bite on his neck, even at that tender age, had filled him with wonder and joy.

Fallyn stared at his chest, but unseeing, lost in her own thoughts. "I don't remember anything like that."

He lifted her chin and brushed his lips across hers. "I know, but I do, and I clung to those memories when I thought I'd lost you forever, even as I buried them under layers of rage and anger."

"We'll make new memories together. Starting right now." She pushed his shirt off of his shoulders and tossed it to the floor with her own clothes.

How he loved that she was so ready to explore this new night with him. "Yes. Right here, right now."

He touched the pretty red charm at her throat, and it disintegrated in his fingers into a thousand multi-colored sparks the size of dragon scales that lifted into the air around them swirling like a burning rainbow.

Claim her. Mate her. Give her your soul.

The sparks shot toward the big fireplace on the opposite wall and flames burst to life, lighting the room with the flickers of red, orange, and yellow light.

"That feels so much better. It's like the necklace was telling me all this time that it wanted you to find it and touch it. I didn't understand until now."

"I needed to find you, touch you." He knew better than to simply push his way between her legs, and he had every intention of giving her a dozen orgasm before he took her the first time. But that plan was rapidly burning up. "I need to claim your body with mine, make you my mate."

Her eyes shimmered in the light of the fire and she smiled up at him so beautifully that it took his breath away. "I want you to claim me, make me your mate."

Thank the First Dragon.

"Spread your legs for me, love. Let me make you ready and feel good." He rolled off the bed and quickly shucked his leathers. He was finally going to be inside of her, after all of these years. Finally make her his forever.

"Stop." She sat bolt upright and held out her hand.

Match froze. Shit. He should have taken this slower and explained what was going to happen. "I won't hurt you, love. I promise. We don't have to do anything you don't want to."

"What I want is to look at you. I've never seen a Warrior's body up close like this. What I want is to touch you."

Match saw his demise in her eyes. Her curiosity and naivety were going to be the death of him, he just knew it.

But what a way to go.

THE FIRST TIME

*H*er Red Warrior must be a God. He had a body like one. Every muscle sculpted to perfection, every scar making him even more good looking, and she wanted to touch them all. Especially the muscle between his legs.

The very center of her, between her own legs ached with warmth and need. His body was hard and hers was growing softer by the day. Put together, they would feel so good.

She didn't know how she knew that, she was following her instincts only, and they were screaming at her to touch and taste every part of him and become one. The moment he touched the necklace gifted to her by the Mother, her fears and anxieties about being with him disappeared and this new freedom burned through her.

Fallyn crawled off of the bed where he'd left her and stood directly in front of Match. He didn't move anything but his eyes, like she'd frozen him with the Blue Dragon's icy breath. She could feel the heat radiating from his skin and practically taste the fire in his breath.

He wasn't cold, he was hot. For her. She reached out and

cupped the underside of his-- his... she didn't know what this was. She'd seen it on all the demon dragons and Kur-Jara, then later when she'd seen the mates fall to their own warriors, but she didn't have a name for it. "What's this part of your body called?"

Match's breath whooshed out and she let go. Apparently, it was very sensitive. Seemed dumb to have something that fragile sticking straight out of one's body. What did they do with it in battle? Maybe it had special armor. "Did I hurt it?"

"My cock? No. Quite the opposite." There was a teasing laughter to his answer.

Oh. Good. She'd seen the other mates kiss this cock bit of their warriors and her mouth watered thinking about it. "Lay on the bed. I will touch and taste you some more."

"Are you sure you're not the alpha, my sweet bossy love?"

"Yes. You are and I am the mate. Now lay down." She really enjoyed the saying she was the mate. It wasn't something she ever thought she would be able to.

"As you wish but know that there will come a point where your exploration will end I it will be my turn." He laid down on the bed, his cock jutting into the air and folded his arms behind his head.

She sat down next to him and skimmed her fingers over his thigh. His muscles tensed, but he didn't move, so she didn't stop. She got onto her hands and knees and examined his cock closely. He was bigger than the other males she'd seen, although this was a close as she'd ever been to a cock, so she couldn't be sure.

No. She was sure. Definitely bigger. Not just longer, but thicker too. Carefully this time, she wrapped her hand around the base and her fingers and thumb did not even come close to touching. His skin was soft, but his shaft was hard. Slowly she stroked her hand up to the top and stopped where the shape changed.

"I am in my Prime, I am in my Prime. I do not explode like an untried youngling." He whispered the words like a mantra not meant for her.

A bead of liquid formed right at the tip and she bit her lip wondering what it tasted like. She glanced up at his face, but Match was staring at the ceiling still whispering to himself. The bead grew bigger and threatened to spill over. Fallyn thought of that woman's ice cream cone, sent her fiery thoughts back into the memory, and licked the top of his cock.

"Holy Hell. Please, Fallyn. Do that again."

He was salty and tasted like smoke and the night sky. She licked him again and swirled her tongue around the head of his cock. She wanted to taste more of him and pulled him into her mouth. His legs trembled and he groaned out something incomprehensible.

This vulnerable tremoring side to him made her heart flutter like those butterflies. He'd said he hadn't ever done this with any other woman. She was the only one who'd ever seen him like this. She liked that very much. This part of him was only hers, just like she was only his.

Seeing his body shake because of her was like the best food and she couldn't stop eating. Fallyn licked him again and skimmed her fingers up and down his cock just to see what he would do this time.

He grabbed her around the waist and flipped her over so fast she squealed. He crushed her into the soft mattress and ground their hips together, his cock sliding over her the soft skin between her thighs. She loved this feeling of her body beneath his and squirmed to move her skin across his.

"Fallyn, fuck." He was breathing hard and his eyes were squeezed shut. "Hold still or I'm going to lose my very last bit of control."

She moved.

She wiggled her hips from side to side, and Match groaned. She loved that sound. The one that almost sounded like he was in pain, but it resonated deep in her chest and made her want him even more. Fallyn wanted her Red Warrior to lose his control, because she knew she was safe with him no matter what.

"I've been waiting for you for a very long time, and I thought a few more minutes wouldn't matter while you explored my body, but I was wrong. I need you now. I need to be inside of your, claiming you, making you mine. I swear I'll let you do whatever you want to me next time, but for now, let me take charge and make love to you."

He reached between them and this time she was the one who shook when he slid his fingers over her skin. He pressed his fingers against a place so tight and pleasurable she was the one pleading for him. He swirled and swiped, building her up to she didn't know where.

"Match." she could do nothing more than whimper his name.

"This is what your touch does to me, winds me up until I'm strung so tight, I'm afraid I can't stand it any longer."

"I...I can't stand it. But I don't want you to stop." Her whole world shifted and became centered on Match and what he was doing to her body.

"I won't, not until you're ready." He kissed her throat, her breast, her lips. "Then I'll slide my cock into you, and we'll come together. We'll be one and no one can ever break us apart."

Magical fire ignited on her skin everywhere he'd kissed her. Dragon's fire licked along her collarbone where her dragon mark stretched and curled on her skin. She closed her eyes and the fire was there too. She was so close to something she couldn't name, and only Match could give her.

"Look at me, Fallyn."

She opened her eyes and the fire was right in front of her reflected back in the light of his eyes and the brilliant flame of his soul shard.

"Look at me when I claim you and say my name." He pushed her legs open wider with his and replaced his fingers with his cock. "Say you're mine."

Match slid his cock over that same spot once, twice, three times until she was ready to cry out that she was only his. He shifted his hips and pushed the tip into her and kissed her, using his tongue to push his way into her mouth just the same.

He whispered against her lips. "Like the bite, this might hurt at first, but I promise you it will turn the pleasure the same as your mark."

Match pushed his cock deeper into her and there was a spark of pain for one brief moment, but he was right. With him inside of her, they were one, and she felt nothing but love."

"Match."

He didn't move.

"Match?"

He wasn't dead, his eyes were still staring into hers and he was still breathing.

"Maciej Cervony, Red Dragon Wyvern, Red Warrior, mate of Fallyn. Say something."

"Fu-uck." He pressed his forehead to hers and took several fast but deep breaths. "I need a second, my love. I thought I was ready for this, for you, but nothing prepared me for how good it would feel to be one with you."

Their bodies joined like this was amazing, but his words, the look on his face, and the fire in his soul reaching out and touching hers, was what she wasn't ready for. It was perfect that they would have to find their way together.

"Match, my mate. Claim me, make me yours." Since he couldn't, she moved her body so his cock slid deeper into her.

"Fallyn, my Fallyn. I've waited so long to hear you say that." Match kissed her again and this time their bodies moved together. Even with both of their eyes closed, Fallyn could sense the fire of their souls filling the room, swirling and twirling, whirling and curling around each other until there was no place where he ended and she began, they were one.

The darkness that marked each of the souls faded to nothing as the light from the other's fires filled in the emptiness. No more would he be alone, never more would she be lost. Because for here to eternity, they had each other.

"Fallyn, you are mine. Mine. Mine."

The rhythm of their bodies broke as Match lost control. He buried himself into her fully and Fallyn could do nothing but reach for him, pulling his body tight to hers as she shattered into a million pieces. Her mind and body exploded with more pleasure and joy than she'd even known existed in the whole universe.

They stayed locked together, floating as fire and flame for a long time. She wanted to burn for him forever, but he pulled her back to her body with a soft sigh of her name. "Fallyn."

"Match." She didn't know why she'd been so resistant to saying his name before. It was delicious in her mouth now.

He rolled off of her and while he withdrew from her body, he pulled her into the crook of his shoulder and set her head on his chest. His fingers played with her hair, petting and caressing his way from her scalp to her arms and back.

His gently touch after their intense joining was the last key to melting the stone around her heart leaving only the golden feeling of what must be love.

"I want to give you something, but if you're not ready to have it, I will understand." His voice was low and husky, just as it was when they were making love.

No one but Match had ever given her anything. "I want it."

He chuckled and gave her hair a little tug. "You don't even know what it is yet."

Fallyn lifted her head from the nice warm place on his chest so she could look him in the eyes. "I've never had anything, not anything that mattered. Pretty ornaments and shiny swords and jeweled daggers feel meaningless compared to something of yours. Whatever it is, if it comes from you, I want it."

He reached up and tugged the cord his soul shard hung from until it snapped. The light inside flickered and sparkled more brilliantly than any shiny ball she'd ever hung in her cave or stashed away in her hoard.

"I give my soul to you, Fallyn, if you'll have it. It's been yours since the first day I saw you, so it's right that you should take it now and wear it, keeping it safe for the rest of our time together."

Not only did her heart melt like he said it would, it's liquid ran out of her eyes so that she had to wipe it away just to see him. "Yes, my dragon, my mate. I want it, I'll have it. I swear to keep it safe."

Match tied the cord around her neck so that his shard right over her heart and filled it back up with his love. He kissed her again and stared down at his shard on her skin. "I've never seen you more beautiful."

They made love again, and then several more times before morning. Once using only their mouths and tongues.

Even though she didn't get very much sleep, Fallyn woke up the next morning feeling more rested and energized than she ever had in her whole life. But she woke up alone.

Already she missed Match's hot skin against hers. She touched the soul shard dangling from her neck and searched her mind to see if the mysterious mate's voice was there.

She heard nothing but her own thoughts. They were loud and were thinking only of Match. Wondering where he was and when they could make love again.

Now that he'd found a mate, he was probably convening a war council with the other alphas. That's what she would do. Because now that all the elements had found their place, the time for sacrifice and savior was upon them. The final battle was coming soon.

The scent of the baked goods promised by the Summer Shadow, Jada, hung in the morning air. She supposed she should go find the others and eat. Before she could even throw off the covers and get out of bed, Match returned to their room.

She was much too happy to see him.

"You're awake, my little *biedronka*. I had hoped to sneak away to get you one of Jada's cinnamon rolls before you knew I was gone." He sat on the edge of the bed and brought the sweet dough and sugar up to her nose. It would be quite fun to let him feed it to her, or better yet smear the hot liquid sugar all over his cock and lick it up.

"Knock knock. Fallyn, if you two are done humping like bunnies, you two promised us some girl talk time this morning." Yvaine poked her head into the doorway. "I'm dying to hear if Match's ding-- oh. Hi Match."

"Yvaine, I don't suppose I can talk you into going away?"

"Probably not." She came into the room and plopped down on the bed. "Ooh. Soft. Squishy. Perfect for sexy times all night long."

Match sighed. "Love, are you up for breakfast with the mates or shall I save you from their torture?"

He winked at her, so she knew he was kidding. The mates wouldn't hurt a fly. A flying demon dragon on the other hand, was fair game. "I will eat with them. You and the alphas should plan your attack and defense straight. I will help the mates decide on our attacks."

Yvaine raised her hand. "Or, we could get all dressed up and have a wedding and a Wyvern's mating ceremony. If I were you, I'd got with that one, because you do not want to mess with Ciara when she is in planner mode."

"Shit. She's right. I didn't realize the wedding was today. I don't know about a mating ceremony, but we can discuss that later. I'd better go find Cage, he's probably freaking the fuck out."

Yvaine nodded vigorously. "Oh, he is."

Fallyn jumped out of the bed and over to her bag. She pulled out the Gold Wyvern's sword. She'd stolen it and the mirror. She'd give that back to Azynsa at breakfast. "Give him this, I don't need it any longer and he might feel better if he has it."

"Whoa." Match jumped up and put himself between her and Yvaine. "Thank you, love. I'll give it to him. Please make sure and put some clothes on before you leave this room, okay?"

She glanced over at Yvaine who was wearing sturdy blue leggings and a t-shirt with a unicorn on it. She wanted clothes that suited who she was too. The ones Azynsa gave her were nice, but red was more her color. Maybe the other mates would have an idea where she could get some better clothes today. Until then, she'd wear her old red shirt and the black flowy trousers.

"Okay. I will. I wouldn't want anyone seeing the naked parts of you that only I get to see either."

He chuckled and kissed her promising to find her later after her girl talk time. Yvaine waited until she dressed and walked back with her to the kitchen where every woman on the planet was waiting. Or at least all the important ones.

"Oh my God. She's here. Fallyn, how was it?" Jules, the Gold Witch grabbed her hand and pulled her over to the table where more food than she'd ever seen in her life was spread out.

"He was rusty, wasn't he?" Azynsa smirked and popped in bite of cinnamon roll into her mouth nodding.

"Yeah, but I bet he was still an animal. Rawr." Yvaine made claws with her fingers, which was a weird thing for a unicorn to do since she had hooves, not claws.

"Oh, no. Honey, was it bad?" Jada set a plate in front of her and plopped extra sugary mix on top. "I mean sex with your mate is never like bad, bad, just like, we all know he hasn't been laid in like forever."

So, this was girl talk. She chose a peach from the bowl thinking of how Match had fed her a bite last night. "I only kind of understand your questions. I will try to answer from the beginning. The making love was amazing, and I understand now why you were all so anxious to fall. His cock is not made of metal so I don't believe it can rust. His dragon was in his eyes, but he did not use his claws. It was not bad. I enjoyed it very much and would like to do it more as soon as possible."

Oh, there was one more part to Jada's question she hadn't answered yet. "And yes. Forever is correct. Or is it never? I'm not sure which applies to this situation. He said he'd never done the making love before. I was the only one he'd made love with."

Every single eye in the room turned and stared right at her. Several of their mouths hung open and Fallyn could see their half-eaten food. She took a bite and opened her mouth and let them see her half-chewed peach.

Ciara snort laughed and had to cover her mouth so her food didn't go flying across the table.

"Hold up. Wait a second." Azynsa help up one finger. "Are you saying Match Cervony, the Red Dragon Wyvern, who is the sexiest man on the god-damned planet, my own mate aside, is or was a virgin?"

She did not have to answer that question, which was good because she didn't know the answer, because the room erupted into laughter and more talking. None of the mates seemed to be paying much attention to her, so she took her peach and slipped out of the kitchen to find Match. The Gold's home was positioned right along the oceanside and she'd like to ask him to take a walk with her along the beach.

She didn't find him in their room, where the fire had gone cold. She didn't find him down at the beach either.

What she found instead was where Match's true mate, the mysterious woman, was hiding.

WINS AND LOSSES

*C*age and his Second, Gris, were engaged in a sparring exercise against his son Apollo and the Gold Master at Arms, Zon, so Match stood on the sidelines watching. He didn't see or hear a clashing of their swords.

His mind was back in the bedroom with Fallyn, and it would likely stay there for a good long damn time.

Every sexy little sound she made sent his need for her skyrocketing. Nope, rockets weren't a strong enough word for what she did to his libido. Being inside of her sent all of his nerve endings absolutely fucking nuclear.

Heat spread across his body, warming him from the inside, igniting the fire in his soul. A fire Fallyn would build even higher, never quench. He burned to touch and taste her again, but it wasn't just her body driving his lust, it was the passion in her soul.

With everything she'd been through, she still wanted to save this broken world they lived in.

He'd like to say he could have stayed as strong as her, fought the unending oppression of evil, but he wasn't sure.

He'd fallen prey to the dark mark on his soul before and only being injured on the verge of death and healed by the White Witch herself and brought him back. Not from death, but from wanting to destroy everything, the good and the ugly, if it meant he could annihilate the Black Dragon.

"Well, well. We didn't expect to see your grumpy ass out of the bedroom today, bro. But maybe you aren't so cranky anymore now that you finally fucking got laid." Ky Puru had been one of the earliest of the Dragon Wyverns to find his mate and had been ribbing Match even before then about relieving his sexual frustrations to improve his disposition.

"Fuck you, blue." He never had and never would talk about his sex life with Fallyn. She and her pleasures were his and his alone to enjoy.

"Whoa." Ky held up his hands in surrender but winked like this was a game. "No need to bite my head off like a demon wyrm just because you couldn't satisfy your mate in bed. Have you tried using your dragon tongue to--"

"Nice try. No advice on how to pleasure my mate is needed." He wasn't going to be baited into a verbal sparring match with any of them. He was too damn happy to let these jokers turn his mood black.

Jakob, the Green Wyvern joined them. "Come on, if we don't get to hear the juicy details of the last holdout in all Dragonkind, we might as well break up the band."

Jett, Neo, Dax, Steele, and Taika obviously couldn't resist the gossip and came over too. This was a camaraderie Match had never had with his brother Wyverns before. They didn't need to know he'd always wanted to be more than their alpha. "We should all be discussing battle strategies for the coming--"

"Speaking of coming." Dax interrupted and glared at Jett.

"Does Yvaine really have to shout ride 'em cowboy quite so loud at three in the morning? It's very distracting when I have my own cowgirl riding me."

"Yes. She does." Jett pretended to be irritated, but the shit-eating grin on his face told of his own happiness with his unique mate.

Neo made vomiting sounds. "If you all are going to stand around talking about how many orgasms you give your mates, I'm taking the other unmated guys into town to find some companionship of our own."

The Black Demon Dragon Wyr was here at the Gold stronghold in force as the security detail while the Golds attended the wedding of their first daughter. They had only recently gotten soul shards and Jett was the only among them who was mated.

"Fucking dragons. What the hell is your son marrying into, Max?" The three Troika alphas and the groom-to-be joined the group watching the sparring.

"Hell if I know." Max grabbed Tristan around the shoulders and gave him a ruffle to his hair. Despite his light banter, Match saw the lines around the wolf's eyes that belied a worry only the parent of a young man who'd grown up literally overnight could suffer.

Tristan just grinned and definitely had stars in his eyes. Probably stars in his pants too with the amount of hormones running through his blood now that he was a young man and no longer a boy. Match had missed out learning of their progressing courtship while he was recovering from the battle for their souls.

He'd gladly sacrifice himself again for that cause. He would likely be called to do exactly that in the final battle.

Match had kept many secrets not only from his brother Wyverns, but his own Wyr as well. All Red Dragon Warriors were told the stories as part of their soul shard ceremonies and were Dragonkind's keepers of the old lore.

Only the First Son of the First Son of the First Son, the alpha of alphas knew the whole truth. Match and his forefathers had a destiny. As a direct descendant of Shara, he was the one and only Dragon Warrior who could right the wrongs of the past. His sacrifice, to save a soul.

What the prophecy didn't mention was what would happen if he'd given his own soul to his true mate. Could she be his own personal savior and bring him back from the darkness or was he doomed to become one with the shadow?

Only the final battle would tell.

"Apollo, hold." Zon shouted from the battlefield.

"Do you yield, father?"

All eyes turned back to the sparring ground. Apollo had his sword raised over his head and Cage was on the ground on one knee, panting.

"I yield. You are going to make a damn good Wyvern someday kid. Damn can you wield a sword. Now help me up." Cage extended his hand to his son.

Apollo held the sword over his head, at the ready to strike his opponent down. The men watching clapped and gave Apollo praise. Match and Dax glanced over at each other. Jett caught Match's eye as well. They three, recognized the temptation of darkness in Apollo's soul.

The Gold Dragon's first son, dropped the sword to the ground and grabbed his father's hand, pulling him up. They embraced and patted each other on the back. Apollo had beat this test in more ways than one.

Match hoped he would forever more and that his own sister would not have to start the cycle of this curse all over again.

Cage didn't seem to notice a damn thing. He turned to the gathered crows, bowed and rubbed his stomach. "Who is hungry? I smell Jada's cooking so I'm about to go get some sustenance in my belly and see if I can talk my lovely mate into one more round in the sheets before the wedding tonight."

"Dad. Ugh. Do you have to talk about mom like that in front of me?"

"Hey. Be glad your parents have a healthy sex life, or you wouldn't have even been born, kid."

Apollo rolled his eyes and marched off the field. Under his breath and for no one to hear, he mumbled, "I am never taking a mate."

Match was sure he wasn't supposed to hear that. Max either, who happened to be standing right next to him. He looked over at Match. "That boy is going to be a pain in my ass, isn't he? I mean, I'd be perfectly happy for Ellie to be a virgin for the next fifty years, but I do want her to know the joy of love with her fated mate."

Match clapped him on the back. "He'll come around. They're young yet. Fully grown, sure, but one summer does not make him a man. Give him time."

Better if the young man didn't claim Max's daughter before the final battle. If they mated and Apollo became dark, Ellie would be sucked into the evil clutches of Ereshkigal as well. If Apollo didn't claim her and give her his soul, she would never know true love, but she would not be the heir of evil either.

The Warriors and the Troikas followed Apollo toward the house, but Match stopped Cage. "Gold. I have something of yours."

"My dignity? I just got my ass handed to me by my one-year old son. He may look like he's in his human twenties, but the twins haven't even had their second birthday yet. Fallyn and the White Witch really did a number on him with that growth spurt. He's ten times stronger than I am."

"This may help restore some of your power." Match slid the Gold Wyvern's sword from his belt. "A gift from my mate."

"Holy shit." Cage took the sword with the reverse a gift from the First Dragon deserved. He swished it through the air, and it glowed with the light of the sun and the gold it was imbued with. "I never thought I would see this again. Do you have Azy's mirror too?"

"I do not. I believe Fallyn wants to return that to your mate herself."

"She will be grateful to have it back. It's the only thing she has of her mother's. She's hoping to pass it on to Izzy someday."

"I apologize that she took it. She had her reasons." Not that even Match knew what they were, but she had used them in the battle to save the wolf pups' souls.

"Right." Cage replaced the sword he'd been using in his sparring match with the golden one. "I hope you know what you're doing. Our victory over the forces of evil depend on it."

"They do, and I do." Even after Match had given his soul to his mate, he understood it was hard for Cage to trust Fallyn. Once she found the Wyvern's mate ring and the mating ritual proved to them all that she was his true mate, they would all feel better. Match needed that to happen soon. He wished he knew where her ring was hidden. He'd love to tell her and have it be done with. But the other Wyvern's mates had to go through the trail, and none had failed. Fallyn would do the same and prove herself to them all.

But just in case. "I have a favor to ask of you, Cage Gylden."

"Ah, man." Cage growled and his golden scales shimmered over his skin. "Don't use your alpha voice on me. I was supposed to get out of that when I became AllWyvern."

They both knew that even if Cage was the Wyvern of the united Dragon Wyrs, Match was still the alpha. "Should anything happen to me in our battle against the Black Dragon and Ereshkigal, I need you to take care of Fallyn."

Cage nodded gravely. "I will, brother. I expect the same of you with Azynsa. She's one tough son of a gun, but she'd be devastated if anything happened to me. We've got the twins to think about and they're going to need her."

Match didn't think he could fulfill that promise, but he would make sure Dax did. "I swear she and your children will be well taken care of should they have need to grieve you."

"Good. Now that's enough talk of death for today. At dusk we celebrate life with the marriage of my daughter. Which is not something I thought I'd have to say for a good couple hundred years, dammit." Cage looked to the sun and the wind whipped around them.

"I know. But this alliance with the wolves will be a good thing for both our kind, and I'm happy that your daughter was able to find her fated mate. They will..." He was about to say they'd have a happy life together. But he didn't know that. Fallyn had called both sets of twins sacrifices and saviors. Zon and Gris thought they had destroyed Ereshkigal's curse on twins, but it was only partially broken.

"I'm happy for her, but I'm keeping my eye on that Tristan kid."

"We all will. Now, let's go find our mates. I like your suggestion of enticing them back to bed before the wedding tonight."

"You son of a dragon. I never thought I'd see you smile. Dirty bastard. I may not have the same trust in Fallyn as you, but I'm glad to see she's lifted the burdens from your shoulders and you're not such an asshole anymore."

"Thanks, I think."

Match and Cage went back to the house and found most of the women in the kitchen. But not Fallyn. She did have a hard time with crowd and there were more people here than even he was comfortable with.

"Yvaine, have you seen Fallyn?"

"Sorry, big guy. Not for a while. She seemed kind of tired. You probably wore her out last night." She snickered and looked him up and down. "She probably went to your room. Practice makes perfect and all that."

Several of the other women giggled and tried to hide laughter. Bunch of horny mates, the lot of them. He smiled despite himself. "Indeed. Please excuse me, ladies."

He found himself hoping Yvaine was right and that Fallyn was ready for another round of love making. In fact, he wouldn't be upset if they stayed in all afternoon and all night. Except for that damn wedding. She'd probably want to go to that. Isolda was important to her for some reason.

Fine a quick appearance at the wedding ceremony and then he could have her all to himself. He wanted every minute he could have with her.

Match checked their room next. Her tunic as still here, but

her weapons and leathers were not. Match's dragon sensed something not right in the air of the room. The fire in the fireplace was out. The ashes left behind were the blackest of black, and cold to the touch.

The fire in Match's soul went cold too. Evil had been here.

He ran from the room, barely outside before he shifted and took to the sky to look for her. There was no sign of her anywhere. He couldn't see her, couldn't catch her scent, couldn't even feel their connection in his soul. Without his soul shard, he couldn't even follow its light to find her.

Fallyn? Where are you, love? Release your hiding spell and let me see you.

No answer, no Fallyn.

He called out to his brothers, this call more urgent than the last and he pull the full force of his alpha voice behind it. None would be able to refuse. *Dragon Warriors, Fallyn is missing. Help me find her.*

Dax was in the sky beside him in ten seconds flat. He didn't say a word, only scoured the area around the Gold's villa for any sign of her. Jakob and Steele were right behind him, moving earth and flora to see if she was hidden somewhere. Cage, Zon, and Gris, flew high into the sky and shined light down like spotlights.

Ky and his second, Taika, took to the ocean to survey the coastline. Blue Dragons could find anything. If she was here, they would find her.

Jett sent his Black Demon Dragons into the shadow, but she couldn't be there. She couldn't. Several of his Warriors disappeared into the shadows around the villa and the rocky outcroppings on the nearby coast. Neo was the first back. He said something to Jett and shook his head.

Maciej Cervony, join me. I have news that I'd rather not broadcast to all that can hear our dragon voices.

Tell me now. Jett was not affected by Match's alpha voice since his line was only half of the rest of the Dragons. But he could understand the demand and desperation in Match's voice.

Fine. The Black Dragon has been here. He has taken Fallyn back to Hell.

Please, no. Not again.

WILL THE REAL MATE PLEASE
STAND UP?

Fallyn stood just inside the cave entrance where the Red Witch, Match's true mate was hiding. She was a fragile delicate thing, nothing like Fallyn. She looked as if she would break if anyone even touched her. No wonder she'd hidden from her Dragon.

In a voice, so like her own, the woman said, "Fallyn, I'm so scared. I don't want to fall to the Dragon, but all of my friends will get hurt, maybe even die if I don't. Tell me it's going to be okay, if I fall to the Red Warrior, that it will be worth my sacrifice."

The Red Witch had no idea she would be Match's savior, not have to sacrifice herself for him.

These were the exact same worries that had kept Fallyn from Match for so long. She understood a part of that now. It was her fears that love wasn't real, that there was only pain, that had kept her hidden for so long.

Izzy, Azynsa, Ninsy, Jules, Ellie, and even Match himself had tried to show her she was wrong. Love was a beautiful thing that made her stronger for having experienced it. Even this heartbreak now, knowing that she wasn't Match's true mate, couldn't take away the healing power of what having fallen in love with him had done for her soul.

She did love Match. But she wasn't his true mate. She'd known that all along. The woman standing before her, with her hair aflame with her spirit, and his Wyvern's mate black fiery ring on her hand, she was the one chosen to fight against Ereshkigal and the Black Dragon alongside her Red Warrior.

Fallyn might have his soul shard, but Lulal had his ring. The White Witch made the rings so that no one would ever question who her son's mates were ever again. Match had told her so. Ciara, Jada, Azynsa, and even Yvaine all wore a ring made from their Wyvern's element especially for them. Fallyn looked down at her own bare fingers in the glowing red light reflected off the walls of the cave.

She clenched her fist and swallowed her heartache for now.

"It's okay, Lulal." Even her name was more beautiful than Fallyn's. "I promise, your Dragon would never hurt you. He wants to love you and protect you. But you must protect him in return."

Lulal's eyes darkened as her fear faded. She opened her arms, waving Fallyn to come closer so they could embrace. Fallyn stood where she was. "Yes. I will save him. I know exactly what to do. I've known for a very long time how to make right what is wrong. The curses of the past will be erased when he and I are one. Thank you for helping me, little red devil."

Fallyn didn't want to be thanked. Her heart would break

when she brought Lulal to Match, but she would do it anyway. After that? She didn't know. She would be at the final battle, if only to help Izzy.

If the world fell into darkness, Fallyn would be home again. If it didn't and the Dragons and their mates restored balance between light and dark, good and evil, it would be easy enough for her to disappear after that. Match was the only being who'd ever looked for her anyway. Without him, no one would bother her. Maybe she would return to Ninsy and serve the Mother.

Probably not. More likely she would find someplace dark to hide away from the world for another a hundred and fifty years.

"Come with me, Lulal. I will take you to your mate." Fallyn turned her back and faced the fading sun. She didn't want Lulal to see the tears on bubbling up in her eyes. She didn't want Match's mate to have any reason to question being with him.

"No. I am still scared of the other Dragon Warriors. Can you bring him to me?"

That made more sense. The gathering of so many supernatural beings in one place like this was overwhelming to one who hadn't been around them much. Fallyn would know. Of course, none of them would harm Lulal, but she would probably feel better protected if she met them all with Match by her side.

"Okay. I can't promise I can make him come with me. He is the alpha of alphas and does what he wants."

"If you want us to save the world from Ereshkigal, you'll make him come to me." Lulal's voice wavered. "Give me the soul shard so it's light can lead him here."

Fallyn grabbed the shard in her fist. The shard could only be given, not taken. Just like love. Match had given it to her. Its light had burned away the darkness in her own soul and made her feels things she didn't know were possible. She wasn't ready to give all that up. Not yet.

"I vow I will bring Match here and give you the soul shard when you are together at last."

"No, give it to me now. Before you leave. It's so dark in here and it's light will comfort me."

Fallyn flicked her wrist and started a nice tall fire at the entrance to the cave. "That will keep you warm and light up the cave until I return. Don't be afraid. I'll be back as soon as I can."

Lulal continued to protest, but Fallyn walked away. She dropped her old hiding spell over the entrance so no one else would find Lulal and scare her. She added a little something extra so that Lulal couldn't see out either. She shouldn't have, but Fallyn couldn't stand the thought of letting the Red Witch see what she would do next.

She couldn't let anyone know she was weak.

Fallyn threw the same spell around herself, and it glittered like the shiniest and bright ornament around her. No one would see her, no one would hear her, because once again, she was nobody.

It took her ten steps before she fell to her knees in the sand and screamed up at the sky. She had no words for this pain, only the unbearable wrenching of her soul, tearing away from her heart, leaving her more injured and alone than any torture from Heaven or Hell. Her tears would not flow, trapped inside just the same as they'd been after her years in the darkness of the underworld.

Even if they did, nothing could soothe her heartache, her torment, this unstoppable crushing blow to the tiny bit of joy she'd been able to scrape out of her world.

A hundred and fifty-two lashes of Kur-Jara's fire whip couldn't inflict pain that compared to this. She could suffer anything, but not this. She could take any punishment, but not this. She could sacrifice her body and mind, never knowing the light of day or a kind word for a hundred years, but not this. Not losing Match.

Fallyn screamed again and again until her voice broke and she had nothing else inside of her to give to the outcry of her soul. Her hiding spell around herself broke and she collapsed into the sand and let the cold surf lap at her arms and face.

Her fire burned out. Even the little flame, she'd hidden away in her heart of stone, fizzled turned to nothing more than a wisp of smoke.

But somehow, someway, she had to endure. She was the sacrifice, her life fated to give up all that she had so that others may live. There was always a sacrifice, and always a savior. Lulal would save Match, she would save them all.

Only if Fallyn got up, searched him out, and brought him to his true mate.

But not yet.

The sun set and the moon rose in its place. Fallyn closed her eyes and waited for the darkness. The sound of wolves howling filled up her brain where the voices used to be, along with the swish, swish, swish of the waves, and the ringing in her ears slowly subsided.

The howls were not just normal bays of the wolves into the night, they almost sounded as if they were crying her name. "Fallyn, Fallyn."

"Thank the First Dragon I found you, Fallyn. Come back to me, *biedronka.* I can't lose you again."

The chill of her body ached at the edges where a fire tried to warm her. Had Lulal come in search of her since she hadn't returned with Match yet?

"Fallyn? Baby, please open your eyes. Gods, you're so cold."

Fire as hot as molten lava touched her lips, breathing the flames into her, trying to reignite her from the inside out. The fire was soft and supple and tasted of hot apples and sugar.

"Match?" She blinked away the ice from her eyes, or it melted in the heat from his gaze. The tears trickled down the sides of her cheeks and this time she couldn't stop them.

"Holy fuck, Fallyn. I thought you were dead. What are you doing out here?" He pulled her to his chest and rocked her, petting her hair, and whispering thanks to the First Dragon.

Fallyn wasn't feeling grateful. She pushed against his strong embrace and rolled away from him back into the sand and surf. The cold water couldn't affect her now. She was already a cold dead husk, and if she didn't want to make sure Izzy made it through the coming trials, she would let herself wash away.

"Follow me." She stood and turned her back on the Red Warrior. She couldn't stand to look at him any longer.

"Stop. Let me fly us away from here. I'll call for the rest of the Wyrs to come back and hunt down whoever or whatever did this to you. Fallyn stop." Match grabbed her hand, but she yanked it away and pulled out her dagger.

"Don't. Don't touch me." She couldn't stand the warmth on his skin, the memory of the way he caressed her during their love making. Not if she was going to be able to give him up.

"What? Fallyn, tell me what's happened, right now." The

dragon didn't hide his fury this time. Flames licked out of his mouth, his pupils elongated to that of the beast, and red spikes of armor-plated scales sprouted from his arms and shoulders. The fire of his anger was palpable. Even if she couldn't see it on his face and body, she would be able to feel in through the soul shard.

She grabbed the cursed charm and yanked it, breaking the cord just as he had when he gave it to her. "I told you I wasn't your true mate."

Match roared so loudly, the rocks of the cliffs and outcroppings around the seashore rattled and cracked, and great stones fell to the ground. "You. Are. Mine."

Fallyn turned on her heel and ran. The waves had pushed her farther down the shore from Lulal's cave and sprinted toward it. Behind her the flame of Dragon's Fire shot into the sky, lighting it up almost as bright as the moon. She heard the beating of his wings and the shadow of his body as he flew at her.

Shadow. Red Dragons hated traveling by shadow.

She used his own against him and slipped into the darkness for a quick blip, putting her out of his reach. He roared again and his great talons snatched at her.

Mine. He roared into her head. His words were tinged with a darkness only the evil mark on his soul could fuel.

Fallyn dove into the shadow again, full on this time, and jumped ahead to the mouth of the cave. Lulal might be in for the fright of her life, but once she had Match's soul shard, she would be able to soothe the angry beast.

She hoped.

The magic spell dropped and Lulal stood at the entrance

peering out. She reached for the shard, the ring glowing darkly on her finger. Fallyn slammed into the stone at the entrance and dangled the talisman between the mate and the dragons she was about to meet in a collision of bodies and souls.

"Here is your true destiny, Red Warrior. I give over your soul freely." Fallyn tossed the soul shard and cord to Lulal just as Match's great body struck the rocks.

The cave exploded around them flooding the darkened cave with moonlight. Lulal smiled, her teeth elongated into fangs, her pupils drew thin, and black scales erupted from her skin. Kur-Jara's dark and ugly soul stared back her from Lulal's eyes. He stretched and a second being emerged from the glamour. Dumuzid, the incubus.

"That's a good girl. Now I have all that I've ever needed from you. Your time on this Earth is done, you can return to hell." Kur-Jara shifted into the Black Dragon and called forth his demon wyrms and Annunaki concubines to take her away.

The incubus betrayer bowed to the Black Dragon. "Now you will bring my sister back to me? Reunite us?"

Kur-Jara shoved Dumuzid away. "You'll get your rewards when I have the Red Dragon's soul."

"No," she tried to scream but she'd already broken her voice and the cry came out nothing more than a croak. One of the Annunaki wrapped its black boney arms around her, holding her tight so she could not move, could not fight.

The Black Dragon laughed and spewed his tainted black fire straight at her. Match shook the rubble off of his body as he threw himself between her and her certain death. The black fire covered him and burned his brilliant red scales to a scorched and charred turning them a dull black. He writhed in pain and roared and growled.

Pain was good. It meant he was still alive.

The remaining Annunaki demons surrounded Match and wrapped him in an oily black net, strengthened by black magic. He continued to struggle, but she could see his strength was already waning under the weight of evil thrust upon him.

I have the soul shard, I have the mate, now all I need is the soul and I can finally break free of Ereshkigal's stupid attempts at revenge and exact my own on retribution on Inanna. I can practically taste the sickly-sweet blood of my vengeance. All thanks to you, little sister. I knew you wouldn't let me down.

"I am not your anything, Kur-Jara." Each word scratched like a thousand hot knives in her throat. He was not her father, he was not her brother. He was the devil, not her.

The Black Dragon shook his head, ignoring her outburst, and hung the soul shard around his neck and directed the nearest Annunaki demon to tie it in place. *You believe whatever you want Fallyn Dragonsdaughter, but think back, have you ever been right about anything? You can't trust your own mind, how can you when you can't even hear your own voice in your head? I have never lied to you. Think about that before you betray me for our greatest enemy.*

"You're wrong. Everything about you is a lie."

I kept you safe from the dragons who would use you up for the power you give them and nothing more. I taught you what love really truly means. Playing favorites and doling out pain to those that do not placate to her will. I rescued you from Inanna's machi-

nations. She's the one who sent your soul to be reborn and sacrificed you to keep her favorite twin hidden. You don't see Ishtar suffering, do you? But that's all you've ever felt, isn't it? Pain and suffering.

Izzy?

Yes, put the pieces together, little sister. There is always a sacrifice for a savior. Me for Shara, you for Ishtar. Would you really be loyal to a mother who loves one child over another? One brother more than his twin, one sister more than the other?

Match growled and stretched against his bonds. *Don't listen to him, my love.*

The Black Dragon sent another stream of black fire at Match and he fought against it. But the Annunaki finished tying the cord and second the shard was secured, Match's fire went out and he lost the fight, slumping into defeat.

The red light from the soul shard shimmered and swirled against the Black Dragon's scales, but its color wasn't as brilliant. The red was laced with a shadowy black light that darkened even its brightest spark.

Fallyn found a spark of fire left inside and shoved her captor away. She pulled the mermaid's mirror from its hiding place under her shirt and ran toward Match and the Annunaki. Without the sword she couldn't direct where they would go through the mirror, but unlike the shadow, Kur-Jara could not follow. He had no way to track her in the light and love of Azynsa's mother reflected by the mirror.

Love could cross time and space if given the chance. The mirror was her only hope. She screamed a war cry and dove for Match.

The Black Dragon aimed his fire at her, and she instinctively raised her hands to block it from hitting her in the face.

The mirror took the brunt of the blow. The fire and Fallyn were sucked into the magic mirror and tossed out the other side of the looking-glass, smack dab in the middle of Izzy and Tristan's wedding ceremony.

A RED DEMON IS BORN

*P*ain and suffering bloomed in Match's chest. The black mark he'd borne his whole life, and his father had borne before him, and his father, and his father, and his father too, opened and drew the darkness around him into the empty place where his heart had been.

The Annunaki and the demon wyrms pulled Match into the shadow and he lost all track of time and space. His stomach revolted, his heart beat so hard against his chest he thought it might explode and he almost lost consciousness more times than he could count.

"Well, well, well. What do we have here?" The Black Witch shooed the demon wyrms away and directed her Annunaki demons to lay Match out on her sacrificial alter, the very same one under the Dragon Tree in the wolves' territory where they'd last battled her and her minions. "Your fiery soul is the spitting image of Shara's. He too thought it's light couldn't be dimmed. That's what having a foolish bitch for a mother will do to you."

Match knew exactly how dark the fire in his own soul had

gone. The first Red Dragon had failed to save his own brother, and now Match had failed to redeem him. All because of a woman. It was always because of a woman.

Fallyn had given his soul shard to the Black Dragon. Willingly, of her own free will. The words rang through his head even as his body rejected the pain of the black magic surrounding him, the pain of her betrayal.

Fallyn, his mate, was the Black Dragon's sister and his ally. Through her, he had fallen prey to the oldest trick in the book. Give the poor lonely soul a beautiful woman that fulfills his every desire and he'll give up everything, even his own soul.

Match had doomed them all by falling in love with the enemy.

The Black Dragon had played a very long game to get to Match's soul. He had to wonder if going after the other Wyvern's mates and soul shards was all a part of the game, designed to find their strengths and weaknesses. their fatal flaws.

Match was the weak link in the entire chain. Him and his secrets would be the downfall of all Dragonkind, and he had no one to blame but himself. Now it was too late. He couldn't even warn his brother Wyverns. If he wasn't about to die at the hand of evil incarnate, Cage was going to kill him with I told you so's.

The Gold deserved to be the AllWyvern because he'd never trusted Fallyn. Match should have listened, but he was blinded by his own lust. Maybe he should have gotten himself laid during all those years he'd waited for his fated mate, then his cock wouldn't have gotten them all into trouble.

"Now, let's see how much I can hurt my sister with this

cut." Ereshkigal pulled out the sharpened horn of a bull and made a deep but careful incision along Match's throat, right where Fallyn had bitten him as a child. "With this relic of my husband, Nergel, the destroying flame, I shall liberate your sick soul and free the evil spirits that live in you, as is my right."

The remnants of Match's fire poured from the wound at his neck and his vision filled with darkness. His own fire was replaced with an ebony black flame, the destroying flame, and it spread through his body, eating up his soul and his mind.

Ereshkigal siphoned the Dragon's fire and captured it in her hands. She danced in the light of the flame and called to her demon to see the prize she had won. "I have the soul, Kur-Jara. Come and let me feed it to you. Vengeance is ours."

A dark sexually charged demon whose powers lied in lies and false facades stood beside the alter, coveting the soul for himself. "You promised to save some of the soul for Gesh-tianna, to bring her back to me."

"Yes, Dumuzid, you and your sister served me well. You'll be reunited soon." The Black Witch lied, but the demon with his black heart could not tell.

The remaining shell of what was once a powerful Red Dragon laughed at the pitiful excuse for power the demon coveted and the Black Witch celebrated. She cupped the red fire in her hand, preparing it for her demon. Why she would want to give its pitiful force to her demons as a snack was beyond him, but that did not matter. Just the fact that she had what did not belong to her, even that she existed outside the darkest depths of hell was offensive. This darkness that dared to venture where it shouldn't needed to be put back in her place and he would burn down the world to destroy her arrogance.

He gave no warning, he would give no quarter. He was anxious to try out his new destroying fire.

He arose as a new blackened version of himself, without the burden of emotion a soul provided. He was no longer Maciej Cervony the Red Dragon, but Sa-Jara, the Red Demon. The black destroying flame burned in him and he would use it to smite those who used the darkness for their own gain.

Sa-Jara rose from the rock and roared, shaking the cavern. He stalked toward the sex demon, the Black Witch, and her Annunaki. They should not be anywhere but the seventh level of Hell and he would punish them all and send them crawling back where they belonged.

Stop, Jara, and turn your vengeance on those that started this war. They are the ones who have unbalanced the forces of good and evil.

Another demon, who had also once been a Red Dragon, blocked Sa-Jara's prey. A Dragon Demon, a Kur Jara.

The Witch shoved her way around her demon while the other cowered behind her. The Kur-Jara had bonds tying him to the Black Witch and she controlled him like a puppet. "Yes, Sa-Jara. Do not seek to punish me. I am the Queen of the Underworld, and a queen does not seek power, only to restore the balance. My sister, Inanna, Goddess of War, is the one you should punish. She is the one who killed my King, because she was jealous."

The sex demon stepped forward when the Witch called him. He too was her puppet. The Witch grabbed him by his clothing and shoved him toward Sa-Jara. "She is the one who forsook this lost soul, her devoted husband for another and sacrificed him to my Annunaki."

The sex demon is tainted with lies and deception. His soul shows his misdeeds in unbalancing good for evil.

The sex demon dropped to his knees. "No, I want only to be reunited with my sister. She begged the Goddess Inanna to spare my life and The Dragon Warriors killed her for it." The small truths in the demons lies were not enough to spare him.

She is the one you covet the fire for? Where is your sister now?

"Deep in the depths of Hell, serving a punishment she doesn't deserve." The demon tried to use his powers of glamour and allure to make his plight sound like justice, but his efforts were pathetic and bitter.

When the darkness and the light were in balance, Hell did not punish the undeserving. Sending this demon to join his sister would be the first step to restoring that balance.

Reunite with your sister then, demon and this time you shall stay in Hell. Sa-Jara pulled the destroying fire up from the empty place in his soul and let it burn on the remains of his heart, then he shot it at the demon. The Incubus screamed for a brief second before his body and soul burned up in the flame and not even his ashes remained.

The Black Witch watched him destroy her demon pawn with little more than interest. "You use the gift of destroying fire well. Turn your fury on Inanna. She is the one who let her own child slip into Hell with nothing to save his soul. Punish her and the balance between light and dark will be destroyed."

Sa-Jara examined the vehemence in this witch's words. There was truth and also lies. He would punish those that deserved it. *Where is this Goddess of War who oversteps into the darkness where she should not be? Take me to her and I shall judge her crimes. Balance between dark and light must be restored. But I will not leave you free to wreak havoc, nor will I be your puppet pawn. You must return to your place in the Underworld.*

The Kur-Jara laughed and turned on the Black Witch, Queen of the Underworld and stalked toward her. Together, they forced her toward the portals to Hell dotting the cave.

The Black Witch stood at the precipice of the gate to Hell and pointed a bony finger at them. "I gave you that gift, demon. It is only because of me you can seek your justice. Kur-Jara. I adopted you when your mother betrayed you, I took you in and showed you the reality of her so called love. Take your vengeance on her and thank me for helping you punish her."

You think you have fooled me all these years, Ereshkigal? You think me stupid? You've used me to do your bidding. You care nothing for my soul, only your own revenge. I have played your games because they got me what I wanted. But now that I have the soul shard and the soul, I no longer need you.

The Black Witch fumed as her lies were brought to light. Her defeat drew nigh, and she knew it. "I don't care how or why you do it, I just want Inanna punished. Here, take the Red Dragon's soul and restore your powers, then you can destroy Inanna and her Dragon, you can end your brother's line, and take what should have been yours."

The Kur-Jara snatched the proffered red flame the witch had drawn from Sa-Jara's own body and swallowed it down. The bonds to his mistress, the Black Witch Ereshkigal, snapped and he was no longer her demon. He pushed her over the precipice of the portal to hell and she cried her lament all the way down.

Follow your mistress, Annunaki, and guard her well. See that she does not venture out of her domain again or vengeance on her light-bringer sister will not be the only I exact.

The Annunaki did as they were told, as was their way. All save one. She wore an elaborately gold and silver decorate melam that caused a physical tingling of his flesh. She approached Sa-Jara and examined him as if judging him, herself. "The Fates will smile upon the sons of Kur and Daughters of Inanna again. Tell my sons that we watch for them and bid them find their mates soon for Ereshkigal's darkness will not be stopped by this war alone."

Thy will be done, mother Ki.

She bowed and slipped into the nether.

Kur-Jara shook and shivered as the soul took root in him. He roared and tore at his own chest, as if trying to get the flame out. The soul shard he wore around his neck flickered to life and red light exploded from it illuminating the cavern beneath the earth.

Kur-Jara's form shifted into that of a boy, then he was a dragon, then a man. The man wailed as the fire consumed him, making his dead blackened heart beat once again. Finally, he shifted again back into that of the Demon Dragon. He writhed and fought against the flame some more but growled and howled and finally got himself under control.

He glared over at Sa-Jara. *Your soul is very strong and tortured, brother. It will fuel me well in the final battle.*

Tortured? Yes. For a very long time. He didn't remember how long, the memories of his life before were gone, but he knew that he'd lost something important, more than once, and it had broken his soul. Broken his heart.

He didn't need a soul any longer and his heart was black and stony as coal. He had the destroying fire and the duty to use it to restore the balance between light and dark. *Then let us seek out this final battle. I have been preparing for it my entire existence, though I don't remember.*

You don't need to remember anything save the outcome. Destroy the light, destroy all she touches and loves, and save those poor souls from a fate such as ours.

Sa-Jara and Kur-Jara flew through the jagged tunnels at the edge of Hell, followed by the Galla demon husks in the shadow of their wings.

Sa-Jara's destroying flame burned a path of destruction to the surface where the Goddesses children lived. It mattered not that the flame would annihilate all those in its path. He felt no sorrow for their pain.

Love was pain. He would save those this Goddess loved, save them all from the pain.

WHAT IS LOVE?

"Fallyn? Fallyn wake up. Where is Match? Fallyn."

A voice, Cage's voice, called her name from somewhere very far away. She struggled and fought to open her eyes, but the light was so bright, and she couldn't see anything. Water splashed her and she recoiled but still couldn't open her eyes.

"Mom, dad, stop. She's a fire witch and getting her wet isn't going to help."

"Fine, you try. But I'm taking my mirror back and she can suck it. Coming in here and ruining the wedding." The disembodied voice of Azynsa grumbled some more but Fallyn couldn't quite make the rest of her words out.

The light faded and the gentle voice Fallyn had known for so long coaxed her mind back to consciousness. She blinked up into eyes she'd known forever, ones that were so like her own. Izzy smiled down at her. "There you are. You gave us all a scare."

Scared. Yes. For Match.

Fallyn pushed herself up off the ground where the mirror

had dumped her and scanned the group standing around her. Izzy was in her wedding dress and everyone else was dressed up in bright greens, blues, golds, and reds. Made sense that it would be in the center of this ceremony of love. She was going to need every single one of them to bring their full powers down on hell to save her mate. They should probably change into battle armor. "Kur-Jara has captured Match and taken him to Hell."

Her words were barely audible, but she needed them all to hear her, to take action now. She held her hand over her sore throat and pushed her vocal cords to their shattered limit. "They have his soul shard and Ereshkigal will--"

A sob, not her broken voice stopped her words this time. This was not how everything was supposed to happen. She and Match were supposed to stand side by side and fight Kur-Jara and Ereshkigal in the final battle. They were supposed to fight along with all the other elements in a force that couldn't be stopped.

They were supposed to push Ereshkigal back to Hell and love was supposed to conquer all.

"Damn it. I knew when Match said he found her and to carry on without them, we shouldn't have listened. I just thought he wanted to get a little more nookie." Cage fumed and paced back and forth behind Isolda... Izzy...Ishtar.

Ishtar. Fallyn's sister. Her twin.

Max Troika, Tristan's father, ran up and waved his phone at them. "Selena just called, freaked the fuck out. There are two black dragons circling in the air around Rogue and the Reserve is overflowing with demon wyrms."

Niko was right behind him. "Fucking dragons. How come you can't keep your war out of my town?"

Tristan grabbed Izzy's hand. "Because, uncle. It's our war now too."

Ellie grabbed Apollo's hand too. While he looked like he was going to jump out of his skin, Apollo nodded. "We will fight side by side to the end."

Galyna glared at both Izzy and Fallyn, the blue light of her wolf shining bright in her eyes. "The hell it is and the hell you will. You may have the bodies of adults, but there is no way I'm letting my children get anywhere near this fight. I will tear those black dragons throats out with my bare teeth all by my damn self if I have to. You two will stay here and let the adults do what we do best. Which is murder the bad guys in their faces to protect our packs. Now which one of you dragons is the fastest and can fly me home?"

Cage shook his head. "Even if the Gold's use the full force of the wind, it would still take hours to get across the ocean."

Niko growled. "Don't you have any dragons in the States? My people are in danger."

"Steele and I were the only ones anywhere nearby." Dax offered the best answer. "There are a few Reds in the west where the ring of fire is active, but mostly in Alaska. Your country is too damn big."

"Our country dear-heart." Jules slugged Dax.

"The mirror and the sword." Fallyn pointed to Azynsa's mother's mirror and Cage's Gold Wyvern sword. "It's why you're fated mates. The light and its reflection. It can travel through space and time."

"Sure it can." Azynsa shrugged. "But we don't have any control over where it takes us. We could end up in Antarctica or the bottom of the ocean."

Had her mother not shown her how to use the mirror?

Izzy grabbed her mother's hand and white light shimmered from her eyes. "Love guides you. You have only to think of your mother's love, the love of your mate, the love you have for your children and any path is open to you."

Azynsa's eyebrows shot up and water dripped from her arms and shoulders. "Uh, Isolda...how do you know that?"

"Sweet mother," Izzy tipped her head at her mother, "we both know I am more than simply Isolda Gylden, daughter of the Gold Dragon and the toughest mermaid in the sea. Though, that doesn't make you my parents any less nor my love for you any different."

Azynsa cupped her daughter's cheek. "I know, child. But let me pretend you're my precious baby just a little bit longer."

Fallyn didn't think they had the time for that, but didn't say anything, because she'd give anything to see the love in her own mother's eyes like that one more time.

Oh. She remembered her mother. Not Inanna, but the Romani witch who'd brought her into this world and given her the gift of fire and the gift of love. The mother who had taught her spells and taught her how to make apple szarlotka. Her beautiful mother who'd given her own life trying to protect Fallyn from the machinations of Hell. Her final spell, to help Fallyn forget the pain in her past to survive her future.

Jett stepped into the circle of people, nodded to Fallyn and addressed them all. "My Demon Dragons have reported that the shadow is empty. There are no wyrms anywhere but in the forest around the wolves' home. We can get you there in minutes if you're prepared to travel in the darkness with us., through the shadow."

Ky was the first to answer. "Jada and I can go and scout ahead. She is the Summer Shadow and can travel there quickly. Besides, she'll take out the first wave of the little bastards with her proprietary rhubarb jam of death."

Portia took Jada's hand and nodded. "We'll go too. Many succubae and their Gold Dragon mates suffered at the hands of the Black Dragon in Hell. We know him better than most. We can create a distraction and then the rest of you can take him out."

Gris and Zon beamed, quite literally, with pride at their Succubus Queen mate.

"But what of this second Black Dragon your matriarch reported? Is she sure there were two?" Jakob joined in the conversation and for the first time, Ciara's calming power did nothing for them.

Fallyn swallowed back the bile rising in her throat. "It's Match."

"What?" Cage growled and stared at the empty place on Fallyn's chest where the soul shard should hang. "Fallyn. Where is Match's soul shard. He gave you his soul, didn't he? It was your job to keep it safe. Where is it?"

It was her job and not only had she failed, she'd betrayed the one and only true love she'd ever had, and all the rest of Dragonkind in the process. She had to own that mistake if she ever hoped to fix it. She'd been kidnapped by a misguided sycophant, raised in Hell, given pain as a fucking birthday present, and almost murdered the man she loved several times, she could figure out how to save him too.

Her voice came clearer this time. "I gave it to the Black Dragon."

Knowing how passionate the people all around her were, Fallyn expected them to explode all around her with a stream of yelling and cursing and maybe even actual explosions. The very opposite happened. They all went silent and most lost all color in their faces.

Cage was the first to recover. He called over Gris and Zon with a wave of his hand. "Lock her up in the dungeon and make sure there are no shadows for her to slip into."

"Daddy, no. She's not the bad guy, you have to listen to me." Izzy grabbed the arms of the Warriors, trying to hold them back.

Cage folded his arms and looked at his daughter with a sadness in his eyes and heart. "Sweetheart, I know you think she is your friend, but she has committed the worst crime among our kind."

"You think I'm not old enough to understand, that because Tristan isn't a Dragon Warrior, or I'm not your First Son, that I don't get it?" A white-hot fire erupted in Izzy's eyes, on her skin, and on the ground around her.

The group around them collectively took a step back. Everyone except Fallyn.

"I know you do, Izzy." Fallyn spoke softly like she remembered Match doing when she was upset. "So does everyone here. It's their unwavering love for their alpha that has them worried and being extra cautious. I wouldn't want me around either if I were them. I've never done anything to make them trust me, and now I've caused the downfall of the one Dragon Warrior they all depended on to lead them into battle."

That was the truth. She didn't like the taste of the words coming out of her mouth, but she would not be a victim to Ereshkigal or Kur-Jara again. She was the one who didn't believe in the love she had with Match and losing that was a worse punishment than being imprisoned while the rest of them went to save him.

Izzy's fire didn't diminish. It grew along with her passion. "The Dragons and their mates just don't understand what you've done for them, for us all. Without you, none of them would have found love in the first place. I wouldn't be here."

Apollo stepped through Izzy's ring of fire. "Neither would I. Without you, Fallyn our parents would have never found each other, and we wouldn't have been born. We should be thanking you."

Cage raged from outside the flames. "Did you not hear her? She gave Match's soul to the fucking Black Dragon."

"Hey, we are wasting time with your little family feud here, Dragons. Send your kids to their rooms and get a move on." Galyna clapped her hands like a schoolteacher.

"Let them do what they need to, Izzy. They don't need me to fight this battle. Without Match's fire, mine won't help anyway." She'd bought the Black Dragon's trick. Maybe everything she was sure of, the future she had seen a thousand times in her dreams were simply tricks too.

What she needed to believe was that the combined force of the Dragon Warriors and their mates could rescue Match and kill Kur-Jara, that they could finally send Ereshkigal back to where she belonged, never to interfere with the world of the living again. They wouldn't do that the way Fallyn had seen in her mind, because never had the Red Warrior fallen into blackness in her the visions of the final battle. But she had to believe that good could win over evil.

Not that it had so far.

Izzy's fires went out like a light in the night. She slumped and Fallyn had to catch her to keep her from falling to the ground. "At least you found it in the first place. I talk a big game because I know I'm supposed to but, I don't have a freaking clue what I'm talking about."

Azynsa came to her daughter's side. "What do you mean you're supposed to?"

"I'm the savior." Izzy sighed like the weight of the world was on her shoulders and she couldn't stand it much longer. "I'm the one who unites the elements and defeats the Black Dragon. With love. I know that I'm Tristan's fated mate, and I have feelings for him, but I don't know what love is. How am I supposed to be the savior if I don't even understand what it is I'm fighting for?"

Silver tear drops fell onto Izzy's face from above. Yvaine stood over them crying, but not in sadness, hers were tear of joy. "I know exactly what you mean. I used to think that too, Isolde, but you know love. Look around you."

Izzy closed her eyes, but Fallyn looked at the gathering. She wasn't sure what she saw in them.

Jada squatted next to the group. "Me too. I was sure I was unlovable until I met Ky. He showed me that not only was I worthy of love, but that it had been around me all along. I was the one who held it at arm's length."

Those words hit Fallyn like a punch to the gut. That was exactly how she felt about Match.

Little flowers sprouted up on the ground. Fleur picked one and put it into Izzy's hair. "Me too.

"Baby, I was so sure that everyone I loved would die that I almost didn't get with your father. I freaking stayed in Hell to avoid him. Hell. I promise love exists. And it doesn't just mean the love of a mate. I love you, your father loves you. Even when Apollo is beating you at video games, he still loves you."

Azy had stayed in Hell for her. Fallyn had never told the mermaid how grateful she was, for that.

Jules flopped onto the ground grinning. "Love isn't all sunshine and rainbows. Sometimes its hard work and sacrifice. Sometimes it's doing the dishes even when you don't want to. Sometimes it's letting someone see the parts of you that you'd rather hide."

Fallyn had let Match see her scars, her fears, her heart. He'd loved her all the more for them.

"Did you even see what kind of dumpster fire I lit up to find my happy ever after? I mean, girl, I slept with half the dragons here pretending I knew what love was." A couple of Dragon Warriors cleared their throats and Portia waved her hands around. "See? But once I decided what I felt wasn't bad, that's when I got what I deserved."

Fallyn didn't know what a dumpster was, but the fire inside of her lit up at Portia's words. For so long she was sure what she felt inside was bad. The worst. When she'd discovered it wasn't, when she'd admitted love wasn't bad, that's when she'd discovered the joy of falling in love with Match.

Izzy shook her head. "But you're all mated. Your mate opened your hearts, gave you their souls. You wear their rings. I'm an inexperienced virgin sacrifice. Literally." She glanced over at Tristan who despite all her fears still looked at her like she was the moon and the stars. "I'm sorry Tris, I don't mean to hurt you, I just don't understand what it is we're fighting for."

Oh. So that's what virgin meant. Someone who hasn't had real life experience and is sure she should be sacrificed. Why hadn't anyone just told her that? They were confused if they thought Match was a virgin. He knew so much more than

Fallyn had about life and love and had shown her how to make love.

Ciara was the last to join the group of women all sitting on the ground in a circle around Izzy and Fallyn. "Isolda. Love isn't a piece of jewelry, it isn't a glowing magical crystal, and it isn't sex. Those things are all lovely and nice, but without them we would still have all found our way to each other. I appreciate the Goddess's help, but love is love and nothing was going to stop all of us coming together in its name."

Did Ciara really believe that? She wore a Wyvern's Mate ring on her finger and a green soul shard around her neck.

Ciara looked directly at Fallyn. "You don't need a soul shard or a ring to know when you're in love."

"Finally." A soft white light filled the area around the women and intensified until there was only light and nothing else. "You see, Ishtar, you do not have to save or sacrifice in the name of love all by yourself. You've got some serious girl power going on around you. That's what will save the day."

"Ishtar? My daughter's name is Isolda, lady. Do we know you? Who invited this chick to the wedding? We're having a moment here, if you don't mind." Azynsa looked around, but only Izzy, Yvaine, and Fallyn had their wits about them, everyone else simply stared.

"That's the Goddess Inanna, you silly mermaid." Yvaine waved at the Mother and grinned like she knew something fun was about to happen.

The white light laughed, and the tinkling sound filled them all with giggles of their own. "Yes, she is Isolda in this life and I am glad she found such a strong mother in you, Azynsa. But when she was mine, we named her Ishtar and her sister Ashtoreth, but those names are old now and I like Izzy and Fallyn much better."

"Ha." Yvaine held one finger up in the air. "I knew it."

"No. Don't you see, my sweet daughters," The Goddess grabbed each woman's hand and brought them in together all intertwined. Except for Fallyn's. "The Dragon Warriors and their mates are the toughest group of heroes and heroines ever gathered, stronger even than the First Sons of the First Dragon, because this generation has all found love. Even you, Fallyn."

The women smiled and every single one of them held out their hand toward Fallyn, asking her to join them.

"I have, I mean, I did find love, or rather it found me." Match had scoured the Earth hunting for her, searching until he found her. "I lost it though. Gave it away."

Izzy got impatient and grabbed Fallyn's hand, dragging her into the circle of girl power and love. "Then let's go get it back."

A WHOLE NEW WORLD

*S*a-Jara circled the small town where he and the other Dragon Demon emerged from under a tree shaped in their form. The site of the final battle was filled with strange creatures, but he did not use his destroying fire on them.

These creatures who lived here were a perfect mixture of light and dark. Werewolves he recalled they were named. Their creator must be very ancient, older even than his own. He would enlist them in his own fight to restore the balance of good and evil, but they were afraid of him.

That was fine. Many souls would be lost this day, a few spared wouldn't make a difference one way or the other.

The Goddess and those she loved were coming, he could feel them in the shadow. He would be patient and wait. He'd like to spring a trap and ambush them as they came out of the shadow, but their souls had not yet been weighed and measured to see if they were found wanting. Sa-Jara would be their judge and executioner.

Kur-Jara was impatient and sent some of his demon spawn

to root out the Goddess and those she loved. They wreaked havoc on the town below, trying to spread darkness, but the wolves weren't having any of it. The soulless husks were destroyed almost as fast as they were deployed.

The souls in the shadow were getting closer and Sa-Jara could feel their spirits. A strange lot these loved ones. Never had he known the elements to mix and match like these had. There was a green earth soul with the shining white of a soul that combined all four elements, then a pair of greens earth souls, a blue water soul with one half of a shadow soul, there was a bright shining gold soul made of sun and wind with a strong watery blue, a very old shadow and something unique he didn't recognize as it wasn't from the Earth but instead from Tír Na Nog, the other half of the shadow was with a two-part combined gold soul, and a red fiery soul with the smallest of black marks was paired with a sunny gold soul.

This powerful group battled for good and for the light, yet they travelled in shadow, through the depths of hell. How interesting. Had these souls who are loved by the Goddess found their own balance between light and dark, good and evil?

Behind this lead group another smaller bunch travelled through the shadow behind. Perhaps being protected?

One of the stragglers had a soul made of gold that was almost completely grayed out by the darkness. He would be the first to be destroyed and sent down to Ereshkigal in the underworld to free his evil demons as was her right.

Unless...there were two other souls who cared for this darkened one. Another gold that was his equal yet opposite. Her soul was almost completely whited out by the light. And the soul of one of these werewolves. Her light was already trying to compensate for his darkness and balance him out. He would watch and wait to see if the werewolf could keep him in balance. The day she did not he would destroy them both with his fire.

Another werewolf followed them, maybe to help his sister with her chosen task of keeping the dark in balance. But no, this one was meant of the one with so much light. Yes, he liked these werewolves very much indeed.

He turned his attention back to the group in front that would emerge from the shadow any second now. He would be ready for them, and the Goddess they were sure to bring.

The twin shadows and their gold and blue souled partners burst forth from the shadow first. Kur-Jara roared and attacked them with his own black fire. The Dragon Demon had a need for vengeance that Sa-Jara didn't like. The fiery soul he'd eaten and taken on as his own was the problem. Soulless was better. No emotions to get in the way of their duty.

But the red fire did give the Dragon Demon Kur-Jara power. Power that the shadows were battling quite effectively at the moment. They were very adept at using the shadows to hide themselves and their partners. The twin golden souls were already stemming the tide of the demon wyrm husks with their light and the blue soul was whisking them away with his water.

Sa-Jara would not interfere. This was simply the normal battle between good and evil. There was no overstepping their bounds. He would wait for the Goddess.

More of the colorful souls emerged from the shadow until only the stragglers remained. They used their elements in a hard-fought battle with Kur-Jara, neither side winning nor losing.

Demon brother, why do you not help me destroy the progeny of the Goddess?

Sa-Jara stayed perched atop the Dragon Tree where he could continue to survey the land and sea, waiting for his own enemy. *That is your battle, Kur-Jara. I wait for the Goddess who spreads her pain of love and light too far. She will be judged and punished if I deem it so.*

I will destroy her even if you do not. She'll come as soon as I injure her dear, dear children. She cannot resist trying to save them from the Underworld as she once was. All except for me.

The final souls slipped from the shadow, unseen by all but Sa-Jara. They had another with them. A spell caster who kept herself and them hidden. Them, he could discern, but she was cloaked deep in her hiding spell. A hunt? He liked the idea of that.

He sniffed the air to catch her scent and track her through it. Apples and smoke. A fire witch then. With a red soul filled with equal parts dark and light.

A flash of his old life skittered across his mind. Sweet laughter and dappled sunlight. Soft skin and a sensual bite. An imaginary castle on a hill.

He shook his head and knocked the faded memories away. They did him no good now. He spread his wings and rose up into the air, the better to hunt the fire witch. She should not hide from him. He would do her no harm. She was the balance he was seeking.

He'd been seeking her for a very long time. Why or how had he lost her in the first place?

Sa-Jara circled in the sky and watched the battle below.

The fire witch was helping the colorful mix of souls. He needed to get into the thick of the battle if he was going to get close to her. He would destroy any and all of them if they kept him from her. He swooped down into the middle of the fighting using all of his senses to find her.

Kur-Jara and the souls scattered as he dive bombed them, fearing his destroying fire, no doubt. As they should. There were too many of the demon wyrms clogging up the battle-field and he shot his weapon at them, disintegrating great masses of them. There that was better. Less interference with his hunt.

No, you fool. With Ereshkigal's Annunaki in the seventh level of Hell I can't make more of my army.

Sa-Jara cared not for his worries. He wanted only to find this bit of fire and see why she interested him so. He still couldn't see her, hear her, taste her flavor on the wind, but he sensed her presence like a part of his own body. She was protecting the werewolves and the two young souls with light and dark marring them. By tracking them, he would find her.

"Ellie, Tristan, look out." One of the other werewolves yelled, shifted into her beast form and charged toward Sa-Jara's target.

He would reach them first. The little werewolf was fast, but not compared to him. He swooped down and shoved the werewolves out of his way. He had no intentions to harm them, but they could not be allowed to stand between him and the fire he wanted.

The light-marred soul shot some of her power at him, shoving him off course. What even was her power? It was not any of the elements, but some great combination of them all. She was not strong in her gift, and Sa-Jara roared at her for attempting to thwart his hunt. The werewolf who cared for and protected her shifted into his beast and jumped in front of her, snapping his teeth and growling to protect her.

He liked the werewolves, but if they sided with light or the dark, they too would be punished. The whelp was new to this world so he would teach him a lesson instead of using his destroying fire. Sa-Jara whipped his tail around and connected with the werewolf, sending him flying into a mess of demon wyrms. Let him fight his way out of that before interfering again.

The light-marred soul cried out, shot a half-hearted surge of her power toward him and then ran to her werewolf's side. The demon wyrms shrank from her light as they should.

That left only the dark-marred soul and his werewolf between Sa-Jara and his prize. *Do not suffer the same fate as your counterparts. Leave me be to find the fire. She is mine.*

Yes, his. That wasn't a thing he should care about, his duty was only to balance the forces with his destroying fire. But she was his, this fire. Why was she hiding from him?

The dark-marred soul brought out a sword imbued with his own light, tinged with the sharp bite of darkness. His dragon shifter form had more power, yet he chose to stay in this weak human skin. "I see the darkness in you, demon. Why don't you come down here and pick on someone your own size?"

Ah, the youngling thought to bait Sa-Jara into fighting him instead of pursuing the fire. She must be very valuable indeed. He would add her to his hoard. Demons didn't have hoards. He didn't have a hoard. Regardless, she was his and he could start his with her.

A second gold soul, this one stronger and wiser, joined the

dark-marred one. "Fuck off, Match. We're trying to save your sorry ass soul here, you douchcanoe. I don't want to kill you, but I will if you hurt my kids."

Sa-Jara growled at this gold soul. He did not like the name it called him. He did not like its threats. He did not like its light distracting him from the fire.

No warning, no quarter.

He shot his dark destroying flame at the group and didn't bother to watch their demise. The fire witch was nearby and he'd had enough of distractions.

Finally, you join the battle, demon brother. Kur-Jara cackled and shot his own black flames at the souls. None had yet been sent to Hell except the demon wyrms, but many were injured, and the fight was intensifying.

Let Kur-Jara think that if he wanted. Until the Goddess showed up, Sa-Jara was busy with his own hunt. If he happened to help the battle in the meantime, he didn't care even a little bit.

"Fallyn, look out. Match is coming for you." The blue souled warrior shifted and flew into Sa-Jara's path and shot ice and water at him. One of the shadows rode in his claws and fired her own weapon of something sticky and sweet.

The weapons stung but did not stop him. He shot the blue down and it crashed to the ground, rolling into a ball to protect the shadow.

Stay out of my way, warriors.

Two green souls blocked his path and as one blew a misty healing breath at him. There was nothing to heal. He was not injured, harmed, or sick. Their mist sank into his skin and the empty place in his chest but swirled there as lost as his own fire.

Get out of my way. Again he shot his destroying fire and continued his hunt. The souls around him were falling fast and many gathered together. Their numbers would not protect him. Magic sparked and shimmered at their center and his fire witch appeared. They were protecting her. From him.

Not for long.

Sa-Jara landed in front of the group of survivors and Kur-Jara came down beside him. *Now we will destroy them all, brother. That should piss Inanna off enough to bring her crying to their side. I hope you are ready.*

He doubted this Goddess was ever coming. This was all Kur-Jara and Ereshkigal's vengeance fueling the battle. The Black Witch was no longer his concern unless she reemerged from the Underworld, but Kur-Jara, on the other claw, did indeed need to go to hell and have his evil spirit freed. Sa-Jara would take care of that just as soon as he'd secured the fire witch for himself.

Punishment comes to those who unbalance good and evil, Kur-Jara. I care not for your vengeance, but do not harm the fire witch or your vengeance will be mine.

Kur-Jara whipped his tail, frustrated at the mandate. *We shall see how you feel about that fire witch once you discover her sins.*

Together, they took the remaining warrior souls down, one by one. Their bodies burned in his destroying fire but strangely, their souls did not. As the warriors were defeated the shining light inside of them transferred from their dying bodies to that of their partners. The soft feminine souls were much stronger than he'd thought. Especially that of his fire witch.

The warriors could not be dispatched to the underworld unless the ones they'd given their souls to were taken down first. That was a mightier task than Kur-Jara could accomplish. Yet he could not postpone in his hunt for the fire witch to dispatch them. She was his and he would stop at nothing to have her.

The last warrior fell to Kur-Jara's flame. The group of soul-holders huddled together, not knowing their own power. He could take advantage of that.

Give me the fire and I shall spare your souls.

"What the shit, Match? Can't you see who we are, what you've done to us? Stop, please stop." The Blue Witch's water poured from her eyes in a valiant effort to help her partner.

"Let me at him, witches. I'm am going to go farfegnugen on his assets. I will cut you with my horn." The sparkling soul from Tír Na Nog marched toward him, but the others stopped her.

His fire witch stepped in front of all the other souls and held her hand aloft, lit with her flame and waved it in his face. "Match, I know you're still in there somewhere. Come back to me, please."

Kur-Jara stalked toward the group. *You can have the fire witch. I will take joy in your destruction of her when you discover her betrayal for yourself. Leave these others to me. I will relish eating every single one of their souls and making it my own.*

"Everybody hold hands, let's take one last shot at him, all of our powers together." The witch with the four elements combined gathered the soul-holders.

Sa-Jara thought she would use the force of her four elemental sisters to siphon their powers, shoot him and Kur-Jara with her shining white light. But when the elements, the

white witch, the shadows, the unique sparkling one, the werewolf, and the light-marred soul all put the full power of themselves together, they transformed, transcending the rules of
the universe, and became something entirely new. Something
no one had ever seen before.

Sharing their powers, sharing their souls. They all shifted
into brilliant white dragonesses.

THIS ISN'T A FAIRY TALE

*F*allyn stretched her wings and spun in the air. She was free. The elements were at her beck and call, the light flowed through her soul. Her white shiny scales glistened in the light of the moon and her heart was full of love.

Whoa, whoaaaaa. Somebody? Anybody? How do you control these wings? One of her sisters flapped her wings awkwardly and flew by. Several more stuck closer to the ground.

I am a wolf, not a dragon. Ack. Is that my tail? Where's my fur?

Fallyn giggled at her sister's attempts to control their drag-oness forms. All but one.

Izzy. The sister of her heart and of her flesh and blood. They two had been born with the dragon inside, long, long ago, before when they were Ishtar and Ashtoreth. But even then, they had not been allowed to spread their wings or use their powers. Their parents had hidden them away for fear of Ereshkigal's dark curse on their brother.

Oh, their brother. Lulal had tried so hard to find love and it had broken him. He hadn't recognized the love that already surrounded him, the love in his own heart and fallen into Hell. Fallyn had almost made the same mistake.

Now here he was again, fighting for that same love, he thought he had lost, or maybe never had. But Hell had twisted him into thinking he could take it.

Brother, rise up and be free of the darkness in your heart.

Hello, little sisters. I wasn't sure you'd remember me. How kind of you to finally show up. I've waited a long time to do this. Lulal did take to the air, but he wasn't their brother any longer. His soul was twisted, not even his own. He was no longer dragon, but demon. Kur-Jara.

He shot a dark and destructive fire at them, but both she and Izzy used their own flames to counter his. He shook and raged and roared at the sky. *I may not be able to burn you down, but I can slice you open and eat out your hearts. Won't mother like that?*

Lulal struck out at them with his tail and his claws, and he would have wounded them both, if eight other white dragonesses hadn't come to their aid.

Get him, girls. The sky was a riot of wings, and scales, tails and flames. Their defense was pretty or organized, but it was well beyond what Lulal could handle. He had to fly up and down and around and around to avoid getting his eyes clawed out or his scales burned off.

If I can't destroy you, I will destroy that which you love.

Lulal dropped out of the sky like an arrow and headed for another dragon who's heart had been turned black.

Black to her white, dark to her light, hard to her soft, and male to her female. Yet inside they both carried a flame that could not be mistaken as burning for each other.

Her dragon, her mate, her match.

Her Match.

Match saw the attack coming and didn't back down, not for a moment. He spewed a dark destroying fire of his own at Lulal, but only caught her brother's wing. He took to the air as well and they fought with teeth and claws and tails and fire.

Kur-Jara, it is time for your vengeance to end. No Goddess is coming, and I will not be your pawn in this tiresome game. Release the evil spirits in your soul or face my wrath.

Lulal never did like getting called on his shit. He sucked up the remains of the demon wyrms, stealing their final bit of life force and fired everything he had at Match. The blackness of his fiery missile was so dark, it was hard to look at, yet Fallyn could not do anything but watch. Time slowed to almost frozen and her world faded to only the threat to her mate.

Fallyn tucked in her wings and propelled herself faster than light itself toward Match. His eyes dragged from the black fire and evil death to her and back again. He saw her plan before she even knew what she was doing.

Do not sacrifice yourself for me, my fires. You are already my savior. Match opened his wings, spreading them as far as they would stretch, knocking her out of the way and opening himself up as a huge target.

No, my love. No-- The wind knocked from Fallyn's wings and lungs as she struck the ground hard. Her wing was broken, and she couldn't return to the air. Thank the stars she'd learned what love was. *Sisters, help. Help.*

The nine other dragonesses flew toward Lulal, combined their powers once again and shot a great fiery orb of pure white-hot love at the demon. The sky exploded as the black fire of fear and hate, collided with the white fire of love.

Fallyn was blinded by the green of the Earth, the blue of

the water, the gold of the sky and wind, the black of the shadow, and the white of pure love. But one element was missing in this rainbow of color and elements. The world wasn't complete, without the red of her fire. The fire she shared with Match.

In the silent space between the explosion and its after-math, Fallyn got up off the ground, pushing pain and fear away. She used the light of her love and her fire to search through the stillness and fog of the gloaming of good and evil, dark and light, heaven and hell.

He's there, daughter of mine, waiting for you. The last curse is his to bear, and only you and your love for him can break it, just as you mother broke the curse over me so long ago. Go to him and claim him as your own once more. The rainbow around Fallyn shimmered and sparkled like a thousand little embers floating on a breeze. It swirled and drew her across an ancient sacred ground where beneath a tree in the shape of a dragon, lay Match, the love of her life.

"Ah, Kur, my love. Aren't you poetic? That's lovely." A beautiful woman, all dressed in white, with long black hair, just like Fallyn's, tawny olive skin, and ample curves stood near the tree. "Come, dragon's daughter."

Fallyn knelt next to her Dragon. He'd gone to hell and back for her and had paid the ultimate price. His scales were burned, his body bloody and battered. His chest didn't rise, and his fire was gone. She laid her forehead on his and cupped his head and horns in her hands. "Mother, can you help me save him again? Just one more time. Please?"

"I can help, I'll always help, but only you can break this final curse." On the other side of the tree lay another dragon, this one also black, but also red. Inanna went to the body and reached a ghostlike hand into the Black Dragon's chest. She drew out a shining, fiery soul. It flickered and sputtered, but in her hand, the flame grew and brightened until it was strong again.

She held the flame out to Fallyn. "Ashtoreth, sorry Fallyn. That will take me some getting used to calling you that, dearest. I believe this is yours to care for."

Fallyn carefully took the flame and a broken soul shard from Inanna and held them to her chest. It sparked and warmed her from the inside out. "Thank you, mother."

She rushed over to Match, but didn't know what to do, how to give him his soul back. Lay it on his chest? Shove it in his mouth? None of those seemed right. Izzy fluttered down from the sky, shifted and touched her on the shoulder. "In one of the fairy tales my mother read to me before I grew up, the princess is awakened with true love's kiss."

More of the dragonesses landed, and as each did, they were joined by their mates. True love healed them all, each and every one. Except for Match. Maybe because Fallyn had never truly given him her love in the first place. She thought she had, she'd tried to, but there was always the tiniest bit of herself she held back in case love really was pain and he hurt her like she'd been hurt so many times before.

Azy nodded. "Yeah, I always thought that was creepy and weird that a prince would go around kissing dead girls he found in the forest, but you know, I guess it worked, so whatever floats your boat. It's an old story, so maybe there is some truth to it."

Cage nodded gravely. "Yeah, those Grimms were messed up. The princess also lived with seven little dudes. You can't tell me some kinky hanky panky didn't go on at that cottage in the woods."

Azynsa smacked him. "Go ahead, Fallyn. Try it."

Fallyn held the flame against her own chest, along with the cracked and broken shard. She leaned over Match and gently brushed her lips over his dragon mouth. His scales were cold, no fire inside to warm them. His great dragon body shimmered and faded, until the cold lifeless man remained.

Oh no. Her heart ached and cracked open, drowning her in the blood of sorrow. Even the spirit of his dragon was gone.

She would not give up, would not quit. She would break this curse. Match had always been the one who initiated their kisses. Maybe she didn't do it right. Hmm. He'd always used his tongue. Now that he was a man again, she could try that. She licked her lips and pressed her mouth to his again. Gently, gently, she coaxed his mouth open and dipped her tongue just in the tiniest bit.

Nothing happened.

"It's not working." The hope she'd had when the Goddess Mother gave her his soul back was fading fast.

Azy threw up her hands and waved the other mates over. "I told you it was weird to go around kissing dead people. Ladies, we need more true love ideas."

Ciara hurried over. "Haven't you people seen the Princess Bride? He's probably only mostly dead. Fallyn, ask him what he so important that he needs lives for."

"He can't answer." He wasn't even breathing. Fallyn wasn't sure she was either.

Ciara grabbed Fallyn's hand and imbued her with the strong confidence of a white witch. "Try it anyway. You've got to keep trying."

The other mates, one by one laid their hands together again, giving Fallyn the strength and confidence to go on. She squeezed their hands and turned back to her mate. She pressed her forehead to his. "I don't have to ask what you have to live for, my big Red Warrior. I know, because it's what I'm living for right now. True love."

She waited and held her breath. She pressed her cheek to his and tried her hardest not to let any tears fall, because that would mean she was defeated, and he was dead. He couldn't be dead. He had her heart and she had his soul. If he died, she just might too.

"Please, Match. I promise to love you and make love to you and make sure the whole world knows how much I love you."

Still nothing.

"What if I promise to make you an apple szarlotka every day from now until eternity just to show you how much I love you."

Did his eyelashes flutter?

"I do love you, Maciej Cervony. I love you, and I claim you, and I want you to be my mate. But you have to wake up and kiss me, so I know you want that too."

The world around the two of them went completely silent as everyone waited to see what would happen. The birds didn't chirp, the leaves didn't rustle, the world collectively held its breath.

A single tear fell from Fallyn's face and the flame in her hand flicked and then went out. Match was gone.

He'd sacrificed everything to fight for the good of all man, woman, dragon, witch, wolf, and child. He died and took with him Fallyn's heart.

"True. Love." The quietest of groans escaped Match's lips.

Fallyn's heart slammed back into her chest and beat once again. Beat for him and their love. "Match, oh Match. I love you, forever and ever. Don't you ever die on me again."

He coughed and groaned again. "I'll do my best not to, *biedronka.*"

The dragons and wolves and witches and even a unicorn clapped and cheered behind her. She appreciated their happiness, but they would have to wait, she had a mate to kiss. Fallyn carefully pressed her lips to Match's and the fire in her heart leapt from her chest to his. The flames licked their way up both their bodies and ignited in a passion for the ages in their kiss.

"My fires. You saved me."

"No, dragon of mine, you saved me."

Cage and Azy helped them both to their feet. There was still more work to be done.

Inanna sat on the ground next to the Black Dragon's body. Tears streamed down her face and the First Dragon stood at her side, tears of his own dropping to the ground in great splashes.

The Goddess of love, war, and the mother to all, reached her hand inside her own chest, and pulled out a tiny bit of shining light. It was so bright, it was hard to look at. The Dragon by her side plucked a sparkling red scale from his own armor, though it was a little burned and blackened around the edges, breathed his own fire on it and it sparkled in the light once again. He handed it over to the Goddess and she enclosed them both in her hands, crushing them together.

When she opened her palms, a radiant crystal shard hung on a cord. The Goddess took the necklace she'd made from a piece of herself and the dragon and hung it around the Black Dragon's neck.

The crowd surrounding the scene murmured and grumbled, a few questioning whether the Goddess should even be doing this. Fallyn shushed them with a reminder. "Love conquers all, even the blackened heart and soul of a once brave warrior."

The Black Dragon shivered and shook, and shifted into a man, battered, bruised and as bloody as Match had been. The shard ignited and the man's back arched, he gasped in a breath and then collapsed again onto the ground. The ashen tone of his skin turned rosy as the blood and the light of his soul flowed through him once again. The red light faded, drawing itself into the shard, and it went dark, leaving the crystal a patent black. He blinked his eyes open and looked up at the Goddess and her mate.

"There you are, son. How I have missed you so." The Goddess caressed the man's face.

"Mother?" He looked around and didn't seem to recognize any of their faces. Indeed with his soul restored, he seemed like a different man "Where is Shara? Did I save him? I reached into the mouth of Hell to pull him back up, but there were so many demons."

"Yes, child. You did." Inanna ran her hands along his limbs and torso, healing them as she went. "But at great expense to your soul. For that I am ever sorry."

The man sat up. "I... I don't remember." He shook his head and frowned. He glanced around at all the others, searching for his answers. "Did we win the battle against Hell?"

"We thought we did, but it was only a single battle in the

war between good and evil. We won, but you didn't. In time you will remember."

"Remember? I remember that you gave all my brothers their own special love. Why did you not love me? Why did I not deserve your love?" His face lost its color again and his eyes grew black. He scrambled up and backed away from the gathering of Dragon Warriors, wolves, and their mates. "I remember what happened after. All I wanted was love and I was jealous of what Shara had, what you gave to him. It hurt and I wanted everyone else to feel the pain that I did."

"You did exactly that. I'm so sorry you thought that we did not love you." Inanna reached for her son, but when he backed away from her, she dropped her arms to the side. Her dragon shifted into his human form and stood behind her, his hand on her shoulder lending her support. "I've made so many mistakes in my existence, but not giving you that gift, as we did your brothers, is the greatest. I thought you would learn from it, that you would grow and thus appreciate the gift all the more for it when we finally gave it to you. I was so very wrong. I hope you can forgive me, but I understand if you can't."

He grabbed the shard at his chest and held it tight. "I don't know if I can. Will I be punished for that?"

The First Dragon answered him. "You'll remember more of your dark deeds as the days go by, that will be punishment enough. You're going to need help to get through it."

"Help?" He looked into the faces of the people around him. People he had inflicted his own pain on. His eyes stopped at Fallyn, and he couldn't hold her gaze. "No one will want to help me, they want to kill me."

"I don't." Fallyn stepped forward. "I don't want to hold all that pain in my heart and let it poison me for the rest of my days."

Her brother backed farther away. "You can forgive me? After all I've done to you?"

Match took her hand and she borrowed his strength. "Not overnight. I think it will take a long time. But I don't want you dead. I want you to find love, as I have. I thought my own soul was too dark and not redeemable. I've done bad things too. I have to believe that your soul can be redeemed, if mine can. Although it will take a strong woman to hold on to your soul, brother."

He shook his head not believing her. "No. No one will ever want me. You are wrong. I cannot be redeemed. How can you even begin to forget?"

"I'll never forget." She had scars both physical and emotional. Both were healing, but neither would ever go away completely. She knew that with the love of her friends, her family, and her mate, she would be okay. "The things that happened to me shaped me and made me who I am. Without the struggle, the joy might not feel quite as bright. I can forgive you, Lulal, because I know love. Love of a mother, love of my family, love of my friends. I know the love of my mate and that's not something that I'm willing to be darkened by the pain of the past."

"Don't call me that. I am not Lulal, I am not Kur-Jara. I don't know who I am." He turned his back and sunk to the ground. "I can ever make up for what I have done to you, to all of you."

"No. You can't." He needed to hear the harshest reality, so he knew how to move forward. "Not on your own. The Goddess is right. You'll need help."

Fallyn looked to the heroes and heroines around her. Many had been scarred by the Black Dragon. She didn't expect them to forgive or forget. But they had all once thought her their enemy too.

'I'll help him." Apollo stepped forward, pushing past Ellie, his mother and father and into the sacred circle next to her and her brother. "I know what darkness is and I don't want it to poison me. I'll help fight against evil if only to save my own soul."

FORGIVENESS AND REDEMPTION

"*A*pollo, no. I can't let you sacrifice yourself like that. You're the heir to the Gold Wyr, for dragonsake." Cage stepped between his son and the dragon formerly known as both Lulal and Kur-Jara. He drew his Gold Wyvern sword and pointed it at the man's heart. "You've done enough damage to my family. I would have you pay for your sins, not my son."

Apollo's arms and shoulders rounded as he clenched his fists. "That's my sacrifice to choose."

Scales shimmered over the features of both father and son. Match had seen these two battle each other before, albeit in training. If they came to real blows, a fight like that could destroy a family, destroy everything his generation had fought for.

Match was loathe to forgive Kur-Jara as easily as his mate. It would be so easy to return to his armor of anger and rage. It would be even easier to turn his back on this feud and revel only in his new blissful life with his mate. He could do neither. He too understood the darkness in Apollo's heart. In Kur-Jara's for that matter.

He squeezed Fallyn's hand and she smiled and nodded at him as if she already approved of what he would do. Match put himself between the father and son and placed a hand on both their chests. "There will be no more talk of sacrifice or saviors. I believed to my very core that the only way I was worthy of love was to sacrifice my own soul for my brother-hood and that if I did, love would come along and save me."

Cage studied Match's face and contemplated his words. "We have all sacrificed for love and been saved by it in return."

"The love was there all along. We didn't need to sacrifice, we didn't need to be saved. We simply needed to let go of our own demons, the ones that have kept us each from our true selves living in love. Because regardless of our deeds and actions, love recognized the essence of who we are, not what we have or have not done."

The crowd around them took a collective gasp as the truth of his words hit them. All except Fallyn. She stood on her tiptoes and kissed him. "Love never fails. I didn't know that until you."

"I didn't know that until you. I would have loved you whether we saved the world together or not. It's not your deeds or your sacrifices I fell in love with, it's you."

Fallyn kissed him again then, and this time it was hot and held promises for even more later.

Match expected groans and taunts to get a room, but when he glanced around, most of the other couples were also sharing an intimate moment reaffirming their love in kisses and soft whispers of love for themselves.

All of course, except the demon formerly known as Kur-Jara and Apollo. The kid had a look of both longing and revulsion on his face. The young wolf who'd become an integral part of the sisterhood of dragon's daughters stood nearby, staring at the ground and kicking the leaves. They were young yet, and with time would go on their own journeys of self-discovery and love. Match wanted to be by Apollo's side to help, but he wasn't sure he could be what the young man needed.

He had an idea of who might though. Several ideas actually. Match put on the mantle of Alpha of Alphas and used his alpha voice to call to his brothers one last time.

"The nameless dragon who has been our enemy for a long time, stands before us now, without a Wyr, he is alone in this world. Who among us will claim him as our own?" Match was prepared to bring the dragon into his own Wyr since Lulal had been a Red Dragon at his birth. But he wanted to give the other, especially Cage, a chance to take him in and begin the healing.

"I claim him." Jett stepped forward, looked the nameless dragon in the eye, and took his measure. The dragon did not cower but did not balk either. "His soul carries the darkness and the shadow as does my own, and those of all Black Demon Dragons of my Wyr. Most of my Warriors are his progeny and also bear no name, it is right that he join us and begin his redemption with those he has most harmed."

The dragon looked around. The Wyverns and their mates were all here and had fought in the battle against him, but so had some of Jett's Wyr. His face took a worried cast, but still he did not back down. He was prepared to suffer his consequences. In the first great battle with Hell, when Ereshkigal had captured his twin, Lulal had set his own pain aside and reached into the depths of the darkness to rescue his brother. If fate would allow, perhaps his brothers would now reach into the darkness to rescue him.

"Are you sure, Black Demon Dragon Wyvern?" The name of their Wyr was a mouthful. "You have had his death in your heart for a long time."

"I have. Yvaine promises that the love of our first-born child will take up that space instead, and I must believe in her above all things." Jett glanced over at his mate and she gave him a double thumbs up.

"Good. If you're going to be a new father to the next born dragon of our generation, you're going to need help. Just like our nameless dragon. Will you accept?"

"He will," Yvaine shouted from the crowd.

Jett rolled his eyes and dipped his head in acknowledgement. "I will."

"Then I call upon all the dragons of all the Wyrs, should you fear the darkness in your own heart, stand and help your brother dragon. Join in the cause to redeem his soul and your own." Match broadcast that call to every Dragon Warrior around the world. Some would join now and others over time.

Apollo was the first to step forward as Match knew he would. Cage moved to stop him, but Azy stopped him. She was one badass mamma and that's what her son needed.

Two of Jett's Warriors came to stand next to Apollo. None had to say a word, their strength and fear of their own hearts was clear. One last Warrior walked toward the others. He stopped in front of Jett.

"I have feared the darkness in my heart since the first day, when Yvaine saved me." Neo glanced over Jett's shoulder. "I know you see strength in me, but I do not, and I need to do this. It eats at my soul day and night, wondering if I am worthy of any woman, of anyone's love. If that means I cannot be your Second any longer I will understand."

Jett clapped Neo on the shoulder. "Go Neo. I'll feel better about the whole group, knowing you will be there to guide them. You will always be my Second Wyvern."

"Warriors. The task ahead of you is great. Not only must you find the light in your own souls, you must find your true mates."

All but the nameless dragon nodded. He'd been alone, at odds with them all for so long, it would be hard for him to accept their help, much less battle through the journey of redemption.

"Brother, I cannot accept their help or their brotherhood. I may not remember everything about my time at Ereshkigal's side, but I know that this will not be the end of her machinations. She will not give up her need for vengeance. You will need each and every one of your Warriors to seek out and destroy whatever plot she is planning to spread as a curse on us all."

The nameless dragon was not the only one who'd seen into Ereshkigal's heart and mind. Match knew this victory was only the beginning. All the more to bring these dark Warriors together and give them the duty to be their first line of defense.

"That is precisely why you must accept their help and join their brotherhood. You will recognize the darkness rising before any others. If you truly want to clear your heart and soul of your past misdeeds, you will make it your duty to protect those you have harmed."

A spark of red fire lit in the nameless dragon's eyes. "I swear my loyalty to this brotherhood and our duty to protect and serve those who would be harmed by the darkness."

"As do I." Apollo held his hand out to the nameless dragon and did not waver as he waited for him to accept his offer. The dragon took his hand and they shook. Neo and the other Warriors threw their hands in on top, forming a bond between the five of them.

Match raised his voice again. "Come one and all, and bear witness to the Black Dragon Brotherhood, and give them your wishes for their success in the battle against the dark."

Cage and Azy were the first to line up and shake the hands of the Brotherhood. Cage gave him a raise of the eyebrow afterwards. "A little dramatic don't you think?"

"Not at all." Maybe a little.

Cage glanced between Match and Fallyn. "I'd rather bear witness to your mating ceremony."

All it had taken was a battle for the ages for Cage to finally trust that Fallyn was Match's true mate. Traditionally only other Wyverns stood up at another Wyvern's mating. The ritual was another secret passed down through the generations of first sons of first sons. Too many secrets had been kept over the years and to no one's benefit.

"Yes. I'd like that." He hugged Fallyn close and answered Cage, but while looking into Fallyn's eyes. "I'd like everyone to come and share in my joy of finding my true mate."

"Wow." Cage laughed. "We should send you to Hell more often. You're like a fucking ray of sunshine now."

"I'll pass." He'd gone to Hell and back for Fallyn and she'd done the same. Once or thrice in a lifetime was enough.

Cage waved the other Wyverns over to join the conversation. Jakob, the first among them to find his mate and have his own mating ceremony asked, "Who is gonna preside? As alpha of alphas, Match did all of ours. Who does his?"

"I think that honor is mine." The tall rugged warrior, with a prosthetic arm and a grin on his face popped into the conversation.

"Did someone say mating ceremony?" Ciara grinned maniacally and rubbed her hands together. "Give me, oh two or three months and I'll throw you the best mating ceremony any Red Wyvern's ever had."

Match chuckled. "I was thinking more like right now."

"Two or three hours?" Ciara asked hopefully. "You do still need the Wyvern Mate's ring, don't you? That surely gives me enough time to run over to Poof the Party Store."

The ring. Fallyn had to find the ring that the Goddess created for Wyvern's mates, to prove she was the one. Until she had it, there would be no ceremony. Match didn't give a fuck about the ring or the ritual. He knew she was his one true fated mate. He had once insisted on Ciara proving herself in a search for one of the rings hidden in Jakob's lair. It wouldn't be fair for him to deny the same thing for Fallyn.

"*Biedronka*, you haven't happened upon a shining ring made of fire, have you?"

Laughter sparkled in Fallyn's eyes. "Ciara, I think you have time to go do your poofing. Perhaps we can all meet back here under the Dragon Tree in a few hours?"

"Yay. One dragon wedding coming right up." Ciara clapped her hands and grabbed Jakob by the arm. She dragged him out of the Reserve, so fast, even his dragon form wouldn't have been faster.

"Girl, I think you made her day. If we're doing a whole

impromptu wedding mating ritual ceremony thing, mind if I make a cake? I've been wanting to try my hand at red velvet." Jada winked and followed Ciara toward town with Ky in tow. "I hear Heli has a gourmet kitchen at her place."

"Fucking dragons." Niko came over and slugged Match in the arm. "I guess if you're gonna be using our sacred circle for your ritual too, the least we can do is provide the libations. Good thing I own a bar. We'll be back." The Troikas, naked as the day is long, every one of them, shifted into their wolf forms and trotted off.

"I hope they come back with clothes on. Those naked man chests with all their rippling muscles are kind of distracting." Izzy stared off into the woods where Tristan had joined his pack.

"Isolda." Azy gasped.

Yvaine giggled. "It was not their chests I was staring at."

Azy gasped again and covered her daughter's ears. "If you start talking about butt stuff in front of my children and I will slap that horn right off of your head, Yvaine."

Dax trotted over. "Hey boss, Jules said she and Fleur could organize some flowers and good weather and stuff. Is there anything you'd like me to do?"

Fallyn answered him. "Could you keep everyone occupied for a little while? I need some alone time with Match."

Dax waggled his eyebrows at her. "I got you, boo. I could use some alone time with my mate after all that kicking ass and taking names too. Off you go then. Don't do anything I wouldn't do."

Fallyn quirked her head to the side. "How do I know what he wouldn't do?"

"Don't worry about it." Match laughed. There were a lot of

things Match would like to do with his mate and alone time sounded perfect. "He's being a dumbass. Now what is it we are postponing the ceremony for. Do you know where the Red Wyvern Mate's ring is?"

"Come with me, I'd like to show you something." Fallyn led him through the clearing, to a small thermal cave near the base of the Dragon Tree. "This was one of the portals of Hell, but now that Ereshkigal has returned to her throne, they are just caves now. This is where I helped the wolf pups and the dragon twins grow up."

Whoa. This was likely where he'd emerged from the caverns of Hell himself. "I imagine this will also become a sacred space to both the wolf pack and Dragonkind then."

"I'd rather it didn't."

"Why?" Perhaps she didn't want to remember their dark times. But if that were the case, he didn't understand why she'd brought him here.

Fallyn lowered her voice. "This is where my things are hidden."

Match's heart skipped a beat. "Love, you're showing me your dragon hoard?"

She smacked her hand over his mouth and looked around surreptitiously. "Shh. Don't say that out loud. Someone will hear you."

He took her hand and kissed her palm. "I swear to you no one else will discover your things. I will protect your hoard like it was my own."

That was clearly the right thing to say because she took his hand and led him down into the cave below. They walked through a maze of tunnels, up and down until he was sure even he, a Dragon who loved to explore thermal undergrounds and volcanoes, was lost. They passed many caverns that had the tainted scent of old demon wyrms and he knew they must be getting close to where Fallyn had spent many of her years on the fringes of Hell.

They came upon a section of the tunnel with small caves carved into the walls. He saw nothing in them but rocks, rocks, and more rocks. Then he remembered Fallyn's hiding spell. She could have mountains of gold, jewels, and stocks in Apple, Microsoft, and Google hidden away down here and no one would know.

One cave had that particular shimmer of her spell to it and he imagined this must be where she was taking him. Fallyn walked through the magical force field and waved him in after her. What looked like an empty room of rocks and stone, was actually a cave filled with shining sparkling treasures.

Along one wall, he saw all manner of swords, scimitars, katanas, daggers, bayonets, and blades, shined to perfection. They were bejeweled and all looked very, very sharp. He found it insanely hot that his mate was not only a collector of these beautiful weapons, but he knew firsthand she could use them with skill.

Besides the blade, what couldn't be missed were the hundreds, probably thousands of Christmas ornaments. He'd never known a dragon who hoarded these little trinkets before, but he could see why. They sparkled and shined and reflected color and beauty in a place that was anything but nice.

"Fallyn, this is beautiful. Where did you get all of these Christmas ornaments?" Her fit at the market in Krakow made so much more sense now and Match was glad he accidentally had a purveyor of these kinds of baubles in his employ. He'd fill whole castles full of them if that would make her happy.

"I don't remember when it started really. I was still very young." She reached up and ran her hands over some of the low hanging bulbs and glass figurines. "The Demon Dragons, Jett's brethren used to bring them to me when they'd been sent up above to torment the humans. I don't know why."

Match understood. He may not have before his own time spent as a demon. The fire in his soul, the one she'd given to him, burned brighter and pushed those memories back. "Because you were the one shining beauty in their torturous dark world."

"This is the one I wanted to show you. I've always had it. Even before the Demon Dragons brought me the first one. I found it a long, long time ago." Hanging above an area of the rock that looked like it could have been her bed, Fallyn carefully took a clear crystal ball. A hole had been cut from one side, and a sparkling white dragon dangled on an invisible string in the center.

Clasped in the dragon's left hand was a shining ring made of fire and flames.

I FELL INTO A RING OF FIRE

*M*atch insisted they stay in her caves a little while longer and she didn't mind because they spent their alone time kissing and touching and giving each other pleasure. She'd have to remember to declare alone times more often. He made her feel so alive and like she could conquer the world.

When they returned to the Dragon Tree, the place was a flurry of flowers and people. Ciara was shouting orders to people left and right. "Oh, good, you're back. I need to steal the bride from you for a few minutes, Match. Go see Jakob, he's got suits for you to try on."

"This was supposed to be a simple Wyvern's mating ritual, Ciara." Match grumbled.

"Yeah, yeah, yeah. Now shoo, go." Ciara made a face at Fallyn that she thought might mean she thought Match was being a grump. She'd noticed that pretty much everyone just did what Ciara told them to, so she went along as well.

"Okay. I've got a bunch of dresses for you to choose from, and here's some wedding magazines so you can pick

8

AIDY AWARD

the kind of look you want for your hair and make-up." Ciara led her over to a table where the other women were gathered. Some were wrapping small bunches of flowers in colorful ribbons, a few were looking through a rack of dresses, and Izzy and Ellie were doing something to each other's hair.

If this was what being a Dragons Warrior's mate meant, she had a steep learning curve. Where was the swordplay and spell casting? "What's make up?"

"Just a little something to make that skin glow, although, you don't even need it. I think somebody already gave you some glow, didn't he?"

He had given her the glow of his soul shard, of his love. "He gave me his--"

"Nope, nope, no." She covered her ears. "I don't need the details of your sex life. Here are the other girls and they'll help you pick out what will make you feel prettiest. I sure wish Wes was here, he always knows exactly how to flatter every woman's figure."

Ciara handed Fallyn a stack of shiny papers bound together with pictures of beautiful women on the covers all wearing white dresses. "Here, flip through these magazines and mark the pages with what you like. I'll go check on the boys."

Fallyn opened the first of the shiny paged books and frowned. She looked through several and held one up for the other women to see. "My body does not look like any of these women."

She looked down at her butt and it was definitely rounder than any of the backsides in the pictures in the bridal magazine. She cupped her breasts and they would surely spill out of the dresses here if the flat chests of the women in the pictures were any indication.

"Crap. We've just exposed Fallyn to the pressure from mass media to conform to unrealistic beauty standards of the twenty-first century." Jada snagged the magazines and shoved them off the table in one swoop. "You all should have been around for the Renaissance. Man, could we eat some sumptuous feasts back then and the artists lined up to paint our pictures, muffin tops and all."

"Yeah. Those were the good old days." Portia sighed.

Fallyn didn't know what a muffin top was. She was concerned though. "I am much bigger than these women. I have... curves where they don't. Is that bad?"

She'd never really paid attention to anyone else's bodies before but looked around at the other mates. Each of them was more like her, than the pictures. Okay, that was a good sign. Fallyn liked the idea of having shiny papers with images of her and Match on them. "Do I need to change the way I look so I can be in pictures too? I want pictures. They're like memories you can hold and see as many times as you want."

Azy grabbed her hand and looked her straight in the eye. "Never, honey. Our Dragon Warriors know what they like, and when it comes to women, they like curves. It's society that's fucked up."

She got a chorus of yeahs and amens. "Your pictures will be drop dead gorgeous."

Drop dead seemed bad, but Azy was clearly trying to comfort her so she went with it.

"Hey, since we're talking about bodies. I have a question." Ellie stopped brushing Izzy's hair and pointed the hairbrush at the group of women. "Isn't anybody going to talk about the whole we were dragons thing? I'm still kind of freaked out by that."

"So, Fleur and I went over to her garden to get these flowers and we thought we'd try flying back. But neither of us could even get a scale to pop out, much less shift." Jules stood up and held out her arms like wings, closed her eyes, and grunted. "See, nothing."

Izzy glanced over at Fallyn and winked. "Don't you all know. There is no such thing as female dragons."

"Don't be gaslighting us, young lady. I was a damn white dragon earlier today and so were you." Azy waved her finger around like a sword.

Another woman joined the group and sat down at the table with them. She pulled a teapot out of thin air and a plate of cookies. "You're not wrong, Azynsa, nor you Isolda. There is no such thing as female dragons. But there are daughters of dragons, who in times of great strife can pool their collective powers and borrow just a little of my magic to take on the form of a dragon for a little while."

"So, I'm not a dragon? I'm still a wolf?" Ellie asked as if her life depended on it.

"You are a wolf." The White Witch handed Ellie a cookie. "And a daughter of dragons."

She accepted and took a bite, which did seem to make her feel better. "But my dad is a wolf, not a dragon."

"Ah, but you see," the Goddess poured them all cups of tea, "any woman can have the spirit of the dragon inside of her. I seek those who are fierce in their loyalties, strong in their will, have strength through the harshest of times, and even those who don't think they are worthy of love and have nothing to live for but somehow still go on. Even in our darkest hours when we believe in ourselves, find the will to be true to our natures, and find joy in the world, we are all daughters of dragons. You, and you, and even you, have that light inside of your heart."

"Whoa," Ellie said, expressing the best way she knew how what they were all thinking.

"But my dad was a Blue Dragon. I didn't know that until much later, but he died saving me in a demon wyrm attack," Azy said.

"Yes, mine too. My father was a Green Dragon who died the same way. My mother had never stopped mourning him."

"Well. I can't do anything about it if Dragon Warriors tend to be a horny lot." She waved a cookie around. "Blame that on their father."

Fallyn blinked at the Mother of them all was gone.

"Yeah, Jett's freaking the flip out." Yvaine patted her belly. Were they talking about her pregnancy? Weren't they all just talking to the White Witch?

Yvaine winked at Fallyn and whispered. "She does that, most people can't tell. I'll be glad for a friend or two, she nodded to Izzy, that doesn't think I'm crazy. I usually just go with the flow after one of her appearances."

She returned to the conversation with the other women. "I'm crossing my fingers for a son with his pretty black hair and eyes. Because, you know, if it's a girl..."

Jules frowned at the pause in the conversation. "What? What am I missing? You guys, I'm new to all this. Why is it bad if Yvaine has a girl?"

Fleur whispered. "There can only be one."

"One what? One girl. Is there like a dragon shifter ban on

having more than one kid like the old days in China or something?"

Fallyn finally knew the answer to someone else's question. "One unicorn. Unicorns are only female."

Jules shook her head and patted Yvaine's hand. "Oh, Yvaine. I'm so sorry. Wait. What? Wait. You're a unicorn? You guys are messing with me, are you?"

Yvaine snort laughed. "I'm going to simply believe that no matter what, boy or girl, the universe, or Tír Na Nog, or the White Witch won't want to break our little family apart just when it's getting started. It's going to be fine. Probably it's a boy."

"Can I?" Fallyn held her hand over Yvaine's stomach. Yvaine nodded while Azy waved her hands and shook her head no, quite vehemently. The little soul growing inside of Yvaine's belly was still too small for Fallyn to be able to tell. She gave the little sprout a tiny bit of her fire, not enough for a real growth spurt, but just enough to keep it strong on its journey into the world. "Everything will be fine, Yvaine."

Yvaine patted Fallyn's hand. "Cool. Now, let's pick out your dress."

"I found just the right one," Ciara sing-songed and swept her way back into the group. In her arms she had a beautiful glimmering gown of red. "I know white is traditional, but...

"No. It's perfect. Match will love it." Fallyn could practically see the fire that would spark in his eyes when he looked at her in this.

"They do go gaga when you wear the color that goes with their scales." Jada waggled her eyebrows. "It's why my all black wardrobe is now mostly blue."

Ciara helped her change into the dress while the other

women put their own jewel-toned dresses on. "I'm glad you like it because Match sent me over to say that if we didn't get this show on the road in the next two-minutes he was going to abscond with you and leave the rest of us to twiddle our thumbs. Well, there were a lot more swear words in his version."

"One last thing and we're ready. Who has something old?"

Portia pulled a gold bracelet from her wrist encrusted with red and pink rubies. "This belonged to the First Vampire and I'm pretty sure he got it from Methuselah. He gave it to me along with a whole other load of stuff. Said he was cleaning house. I'd like you to have it."

"Thank you, Queen Portia."

"Something new?"

"Oh. I made this while we were decorating." Yvaine pulled out a ring of flowers woven into a small circlet. "It's a garter. I mean, I was gonna make Jett pull off my thigh later, but I'm willing to sacrifice in the name of the mating ritual."

Yvaine ducked beneath Fallyn's dress and latched the garter around her leg just above her knee.

"Okay, we're on a roll. Something borrowed?"

Isolda and Azynsa exchanged looks. "Give it to her, mom. It's only borrowed, not stolen this time."

Azynsa reached into a bag on her hip and brought out her mother's golden hand mirror. "I want it back this time, sister."

She turned Fallyn around and slid the mirror into the back of the dress.

"Something blue." They all looked at Jada.

"Umm, All I've got is my t-shirt, or my panties, but that's weird and also they say, 'Talk Kiwi to me' on them and that would probably piss both Match and Ky off."

"Here." Fleur took the bouquet of roses she'd put together and gently stroked the petals. They turned a pretty shade of light blue before their very eyes. "That should do it."

Fallyn's heart felt full to overflowing. "Thank you all for that pre-mating ritual. I will cherish it always."

She gave each of them a hug and told them how much they meant to her. Everyone had a tear or two by the time she was done. Ciara most of all. "I love crying at weddings, I mean mating rituals. Let's get you hitched, or rather mated."

The women formed a line, with Fallyn at the back, which she loved, because she got to watch each of their mate's eyes glow with a light as they joined them in a circle around the Dragon Tree.

When Ciara joined Jakob and Fallyn was the only one left, she finally saw Match waiting for her, like he'd been his entire life. He was dressed in a black outfit as were the other dragons, but his shirt was a beautiful fiery shade of red. It matched the fire in his eyes as he looked adoringly at her.

Match, her mate, and love for all time. His smile was radiant, and he held out his hand to call her to his side.

She walked down the aisle of green grass, red flowers growing at her feet with each step. The wind blew through her hair and golden light from the sun shined down on her. She could hear the ocean and taste its brine in the air. There was no place more perfect on the Earth for binding herself to her warrior for all to see.

And at the base of the tree stood the First Dragon and the White Witch. The mother and father she'd never really known, but that she loved and who loved her just the same. Kur kissed her lightly on the cheek and then opened an ancient book. He found the pages he was looking for right away and began the ritual.

He read from the book for all to hear, but Fallyn wasn't paying attention. She could only see, hear, smell, taste, and feel Match. He stared down at her with so much love that the fire inside of them both flickered across their skin, sharing in the union of their souls.

The First Dragon put her hand and Match's on the open book. "Fallyn, repeat after me."

"*Ni*, Fallyn Ejderhanınkizi *cad men anna ni gud* Maciej Cervony." The cadence of the sentence felt oddly familiar. She'd heard something similar to it before, but she couldn't quite put her finger on when or where.

She repeated the words and they flowed off of her tongue as if it was her native language. "*Ni*, Fallyn Ejderhanınkizi, *cad men anna ni gud* Maciej Cervony.

She didn't need any translation, the meaning of the words rang in her mind as she said them. *I, Fallyn Dragonsdaughter, bind myself to you warrior, Maciej Cervony.*

As she finished the sentence, Match took her hand and slid the ring of fire onto her finger. The fire in her own soul danced and celebrated, understanding how this sacred ritual marked the joining of their lives.

Match said his vow back to her. "*Ni*, Maciej Cervony, *gud tammabuki, cad men anna ni ilati sinnis*, Fallyn Ejderhanınkizi."

I, Maciej Cervony, bind myself to you goddess of my heart, Fallyn Dragonsdaughter.

"I now declare you fated and mated. You may kiss the bejeebers out of her. And might I recommend a dozen or so orgasms later." The First Dragon winked and shimmered shifting into his dragon form and took to the sky.

He loopty-looped above their heads, raining a sparkling rainbow of shimmering scales like fireworks in the sky.

Match grabbed Fallyn in his arms and kissed her so passionately that the world around them fell away. There was only her and her mate, their fire, their love, and their happily ever after.

―――――――

NOT READY FOR the story to be over?

Get a bonus epilogue for Match and Fallyn available only to my Curvy Connection email list.

Not on the list yet, join here and get Match and Fallyn's epilogue right away—> https://geni.us/MatchandFallynEpilogue

NOT READY FOR the Dragons Love Curves series to be over?

Me either, get Tamed, book one in the new Black Dragon Brotherhood series for more dragon shifter and curvy girl stories now.

DEAR READER

My dearest reader,

Years ago when I first set out the write the Dragons Love Curves series, it was just supposed to be four books. Ha Ha Ha.

Even from the very beginning, I knew bits of Match and Fallyn's story. I wrote a prologue to their book, knowing even back then that that their story would be the last in the series.

If you're reading this, you likely went on the lovely long journey of all the Dragon Warriors, their mates, and sifted through the bajillions of clues I dropped for not only this final couple's story, but the real nature of the relationship between the Goddess Inanna and the Black Dragon and, of course the transformative power of love.

I wanted to know where the in literature the very first time a Dragon was mentioned. Turns out one of the world's first authors was a woman named Enheduanna. One of her most well-known stories was the Descent of Inanna into the Underworld, also known as Kur.

One lesser known translation of the word Kur is dragon.

I borrowed a lot of the concepts for the Dragon's culture from Sumerian mythology. Inanna really is the Sumerian goddess of love and war, but also prostitution, fertility, sensuality, and procreation. The story of her descent into the underworld and her return, is filled with all kinds of bizarreness.

I had a lot of fun taking the characters and making my own story from these thousands of years old story.

I do hope you aren't too disappointed that our White Witch isn't infallible. No mother ever is. But she wanted very badly to make amends.

I also considered for a long time what to do about the Black Dragon. He was such a bad guy, but the worst villains are the ones with the worst back stories, and at his core, all he really wanted was love.

I couldn't kill him. I just couldn't.

So I'm giving him the chance to be redeemed.

The Dragons Love Curves series may be over, but the stories of the Black Dragon Brotherhood are just beginning.

I hope you'll come on the next adventure for the Dragons and their curvy girls with me in the first book in series - Tamed.

If you need more curvy girls getting their happy ever afters with hunky guys, come on over and join my email list, the Curvy Connection so we can hang out in between books too.

Lots of hugs from me to you,

—Aidy

ACKNOWLEDGMENTS

I had a lot of help getting this book finished and published for you.

Lots of thanks are coming your way.

Thanks to the ladies of Colorado Romance Writers who helped me brainstorm when I got stuck on the points of the plot. McKenna and McKenzie Rogue, Zoey Indiana, Michelle Ziegler, Zoey Indiana, Dawn McGray, DL Potter, Holly Roberds, and Anna Michael.

I'm not good at asking for help, and you helped me anyway.

I might not have actually finished the book if not for the Level Up Romance Writers sprint chats and the amazing writers who stayed up late with me to get words on the page. Brittany, Kathy, Merri, Ivy, Claire, Dylann, Tiffany, Zoey, and all the other romance writers who popped in to write - wheeee! Can't wait to write all the words with you all again.

My readers are the bestest of the best.

Lots of hugs to Frania, Helena, Liz, and Cheryl for getting excited about re-reading the whole series to scour for clues about Match and Fallyn's story and sent me your notes and theories. Fallyn and Izzy are twins because of your suggestion.

Thanks to Linda, Corinne, Theresa, and Michelle for keeping the Amazeballs going when I had to ban myself from the internet to get this book finished. Mwah.

Finally, I have the utmost gratitude to Ann Bopp, Tracey Appling, Daphine Gooch, Missy Garner, Jennifer Anderson and Dorothy Billmeier for last minute proofreading. Any remaining errors are Uno the Naughty Kitty's fault because he stuck his butt in my face while I was writing.

ALSO BY AIDY AWARD

The Curvy Love Series

Curvy Diversion

Curvy Temptation

Curvy Persuasion

The Curvy Seduction Saga

Rebound

Rebellion

Reignite

Dragons Love Curves

Chase Me

Tease Me

Unmask Me

Bite Me

Cage Me

Baby Me

Defy Me

Surprise Me

Dirty Dragon

Crave Me

Slay Me

Alpha Wolves Want Curves

Dirty Wolf

Naughty Wolf

Kinky Wolf

ABOUT THE AUTHOR

Aidy Award is a curvy girl who kind of has a thing for stormtroopers. She's also the author of the popular Curvy Love series and the hot new Dragons Love Curves series. She writes curvy girl erotic romance, about real love, and dirty fun, with happy ever afters because every woman deserves great sex and even better romance, no matter her size, shape, or what the scale says.

Read the delicious tales of hot heroes and curvy heroines come to life under the covers and between the pages of Aidy's books. Then let her know because she really does want to hear from her readers.

Connect with Aidy on her website. www.AidyAward.com get her Curvy Connection, and join her Facebook Group - Aidy's Amazeballs.

Printed in Great Britain
by Amazon

43407512R00135